'Don't you ever smile?' Zachary murmured, and to her shock she felt his finger brush her mouth, a featherlight touch that sent heat rushing through her whole body.

'Don't!' Maddie gasped, jerking her head away as if the touch had been an unbearable intrusion, and he stared down at her, his brows rising.

'Well, well,' he drawled, smiling. 'Who'd have thought it?'

'Who'd have thought what?' She was trying to understand why she had reacted like that to a mere gesture.

'And I had you down as the sophisticated kind,' he murmured, looking so amused she could have hit him.

'As you've only just met me, I don't see how you could have me down as anything at all!' she snapped, eyeing him with dislike.

'It must be your job,' he said. 'It had me fooled, I suppose. The kind of music you like, your voice, what you said on the air last night—it all added up to a certain image.'

'I've heard that before,' Maddie said scornfully. 'From men on the make. Well, I'm not available!'

Books you will enjoy
by CHARLOTTE LAMB

WHIRLWIND
Anna knew that men like Laird Montgomery were dangerous. But, however hard she tried to avoid him, their paths seemed destined to cross. She had to admit that she didn't entirely mind—until she found out that she couldn't trust him . . .

ECHO OF PASSION
Zoe had been hurt by Rory Ormond before, and she was determined to stop the same thing happening to another young girl. She believed she had got over their affair and was strong enough to thwart Rory's plans without danger to her own emotions. Until she met him again . . .

OUT OF CONTROL
When she was marooned in her fog-bound cottage with an infuriatingly mocking man, Liza's well-ordered emotions threatened to let her down. Despite his attraction, Liza was determined to resist Keir Zachary, sure that it was all a game to him. But it was a game that could consume them both in its passionate flames . . .

YOU CAN LOVE A STRANGER

BY

CHARLOTTE LAMB

MILLS & BOON LIMITED
ETON HOUSE   18-24 PARADISE ROAD
RICHMOND   SURREY   TW9 1SR

All the characters in this book have no existence outside the imagination of the Author, and have no relation whatsoever to anyone bearing the same name or names. They are not even distantly inspired by any individual known or unknown to the Author, and all the incidents are pure invention.

All Rights Reserved. The text of this publication or any part thereof may not be reproduced or transmitted in any form or by any means, electronic or mechanical, including photocopying, recording, storage in an information retrieval system, or otherwise, without the written permission of the publisher.

This book is sold subject to the condition that it shall not, by way of trade or otherwise, be lent, resold, hired out or otherwise circulated without the prior consent of the publisher in any form of binding or cover other than that in which it is published and without a similar condition including this condition being imposed on the subsequent purchaser.

First published in Great Britain 1988
by Mills & Boon Limited

© Charlotte Lamb 1988

Australian copyright 1988
Philippine copyright 1988
This edition 1988

ISBN 0 263 75994 6

Set Baskerville 11 on 12pt.
01-0688-56385

Typeset in Great Britain by JCL Graphics, Bristol

Printed and bound in Great Britain by
Collins, Glasgow

CHAPTER ONE

'EVER been in love, Maddie?' Con asked, finishing his drink in one swallow.

How much more was he going to drink? thought Maddie without replying, her grey eyes anxious. He had been drinking when she had arrived. She had halted to look into a mirror, pretending to check on her newly razor-cut black hair and the set of her white Puritan collar. In fact she had been watching Con and worrying about him.

He had hardly eaten anything. The waiter had whisked away his plate with an offended sniff. 'Was there something wrong with the steak, sir?'

'No, just something wrong with me,' Con had glowered. He did a lovely glower. It was easy for him because he had such heavy black brows over his hazel eyes. Surprisingly, he had blond hair, too. The combination was absolutely natural, a freak of genetics, and somehow it was typical of Con that he should surprise on sight. He was a surprising man in other ways, too, and Maddie liked him enough to wish he would stop brooding and drinking and talking about love.

'Love,' he said from time to time, laughing angrily. 'To hell with it, that's what I say. A fool's game. Isn't that right, Maddie?'

She kept saying soothingly 'Absolutely, Con. Love's a fool's game,' but he wasn't listening, anyway.

'We need another bottle,' he said now, looking round for the wine waiter.

'I'll have to be going soon, don't bother for me,' Maddie hurriedly said, frowning. 'Just coffee, thanks,' she told the waiter.

'And liqueurs, then,' added Con.

She had never heard a whisper about him having a drink problem, although she had heard a great deal about him during the six months since she started working at the radio station. Everyone seemed to know all about Con Osborne's private life—in fact, he didn't really have a private life. He was far too public a figure in this town. People considered him to be their property; they were fascinated by everything about him—he was their most famous resident, their richest, too. They couldn't talk of anything else. Join any group of more than two people and you could bet your last dollar that they would be talking about Con.

It was true that he was a larger-than-life character —even if he wasn't large in any other sense. Con was not a tall man, nor a big one; he was only five foot seven inches, and distinctly skinny and slightly built.

In fact, Maddie had wondered if it was his lack of height that had given him so much aggressive drive? A desire to compensate, force people to respect him? She had thought of other small men—Napoleon, for instance. Short and pushy men who wanted to conquer the world were always popping up in the history books, and Con was a stormy man with some tremendous achievements behind him already. Maddie had not realised how young he was until she came to Seaborough and met him for that first interview. She had heard on the grapevine about his rapid expansion of the small family business he had inherited when he was twenty-two, but she hadn't realised that he was even now barely thirty. He had given her a thorough grilling that first day, and come over as an energetic, driven man. Maddie hadn't been sure she liked him, but working with a man taught you a great deal about him and she respected Con, she had a lot of to time for him. It worried her to see him drink as if the stuff had just been invented.

'Brandy? *Crème de menthe?*' he suggested as the wine waiter filled his glass with golden brandy.

'Not for me, I'm working tonight, remember?' she said.

The wine waiter left and Con held the brandy glass in one hand, expertly swirling the alcohol while he stared into its rich amber depths. 'Here's to divorce,' he said and drank, his head tilting.

He wasn't good-looking exactly, but he had good bones and a look about him that made women interested, and it wasn't just his money they wanted. Con had a sex appeal that came from the same source as his business success; he had a vibrant personality and fierce drive. Not for the first time, Maddie wondered why his wife had left him—the marriage had lasted just over a year, she had been told, hardly worth the marriage licence, she thought. She hadn't met his wife, but they said Jill Osborne was beautiful, and Maddie could well believe it. Con liked the best; he *would* pick a beautiful woman.

Maddie didn't need a mirror to tell her that she herself wasn't beautiful; she had known it all her life and resented it because she had a very beautiful older sister. People looked from one to the other of them and couldn't believe she and Penny *were* sisters. Penny was tall and shapely, with a cameo face and vivid blue eyes. By the time Maddie reached her teens she was skinny, angular, with untidy black hair and nondescript grey eyes. She had nothing going for her, and refused to be Penny's bridesmaid at her sister's wedding. Oh, Penny had talked her into it in the end, but Maddie had felt like wearing a bag over her head as they walked down the aisle.

She had grown out of that angry resentment, of course; she had acquired a sense of herself, a style of her own—she had learnt how to make men look twice. It was all a matter of confidence: if you first made sure you looked your best and walked into a room being sure about that, you could attract people by that very air of confidence. People liked optimism; a sparkle of it caught their eye.

Maddie had had several men in her life who had almost fallen in love with her, and with whom she had almost been in love, but for some reason it had never happened. So when she left London and got this job with the radio station at Seaborough she hadn't missed anyone. Everyone had said leaving London would be a mistake; she'd be bored and hate the sea and the country, life in a little resort town where winter dragged on for six months and summer was a crazy time of visitors and candy-floss and kiss-me-quick booths on the pier. Maddie had missed her family, and she kept in close touch with them because they were a close family, but she hadn't missed anything else. She loved it here.

They were a friendly lot in Seaborough, and, because they were such a small, enclosed society, they all seemed gregarious and sociable, always eating out, always having parties. She had been to quite a few and seen Con at them. He had been born here; he knew everyone, just as they all knew him. He might employ a lot of them, either on his two weekly newspapers, or on his radio station, or at one of the newsagent's shops he owned—but that did not mean he lived on another plane or expected to be treated as someone special. They all knew he was someone special, of course. But they called him Con and he used their first names. It was a matter of principle with them all, a declaration of independence Con respected and accepted.

That was why Maddie liked him—she admired his attitudes and found him easy to work for. She had been surprised when he'd asked her out to dinner; this was the first time they had had a date, but she had understood why he couldn't bear to be alone tonight. He had been frank about that; Con was direct almost to the point of being rude.

'I'll go out of my mind if I'm alone tonight. Have dinner with me and help me keep my sanity.' He had grinned, but it had not really been a joke. His eyes had been angry, full of pain. His divorce would soon be final; his marriage was nearly over. Con was still hurting.

By tomorrow, everyone would know that she had had dinner with him and they would all know why he was drinking heavily, but they would still be curious, and she hoped they wouldn't ask too many questions. She wouldn't answer them, of course, but the endless fencing and evasion would be a bore she would rather do without. Not that Con had told her much; they hadn't talked of anything personal, she had had to read between the actual words to guess what was in his mind, but his eyes had been the real betrayal, and Maddie felt very sorry for him.

'Do you ever wish tomorrow would never come, Maddie?' he asked now, finishing his brandy and looking round for another one. The wine waiter heard the click of his finger and thumb and appeared at once.

'I must go,' Maddie said hurriedly. 'I'm on the air in just under an hour, remember?' She had already been in to the studio to set up all her discs and work out a vague running script, or rather her own version of that, a few roughly scribbled notes on which she would elaborate on the air. She only had to sit down and check out everything before transmission time, but she had to leave now to have time for that.

'Yes, OK,' Con reluctantly agreed, asking for the bill.

The restaurant was a short walk from the radio

station; uphill all the way, though. It had been an easy walk down, but it was not so much fun going back up the steep, narrow streets winding round and round between eighteenth-century workmen's cottages; fashionable now and much sought after, they had all been done up; pastel-washed in pinks and creams and lavenders, they were mysterious in the moonlight.

'Thanks for putting up with me tonight,' Con said, his eyes brooding on the moon, as if it had no business to shine when he was unhappy.

'I enjoyed the evening very much.' It was less than the truth; she had several times wished the evening was over, for Con's unhappiness was unbearable to watch.

'I couldn't have been alone. I'm too tense.' He wasn't listening to her; he had hardly known who she was all evening. Con was living inside his own head and hating his thoughts. You couldn't really blame him—it wasn't merely that his wife had run off with another man, it must hurt even more that she had picked his own brother! Con had lost more than a wife; his family life had been wrecked overnight by two betrayals.

'Just get a good night's sleep,' she comforted, and he laughed.

'I shan't sleep!' He was still staring at the sky and broke out, 'Not with that damned moon shining in the window all night!' He looked down into Maddie's concerned face then, and muttered between grim lips, 'I don't want to see her again. I don't know if I can stand it!'

'Haven't you seen her since she left?' Maddie blurted out, then realised she shouldn't have asked anything. Con was white.

'I saw her in court, during the divorce hearing. We didn't speak—*he* was with her.'

His own brother! thought Maddie, watching him and wishing she could think of something to say that would really help.

'If he's with her tomorrow, I'll throw him out of my house,' Con snarled, lips curling back from his teeth, then he ran a hand over his face to hide it from her. 'Tomorrow is going to be one long endurance test.'

'Do you have to go?' Maddie asked, because she felt she had to say something.

'What?' He let his hand drop and stared, stopping in his tracks.

'Well . . .' She started stammering, wishing he didn't look so black and angry. 'I mean, can't somebody else go?'

'Somebody else?' he repeated, apparently having difficulty grasping the suggestion.

They were standing still in the silent street; the houses around them were mostly dark, their roofs silver with moonlight. People here went to bed early unless they were night-workers, when they switched on the radio and listened to her. She had been quite surprised by the number of listeners she had; the town always seemed to be dead by midnight, yet her show went on the air then and a lot of people tuned into it.

'We're meeting the auctioneer at the house to

decide what goes into the sale and what each of us wants to keep,' Con explained. 'Our lawyers insisted on it as part of the financial settlement, so that there can be no argument later.'

From what Maddie had heard, Jill Osborne had been neither greedy nor vindictive; she hadn't demanded enormous alimony, but then, people said cynically, she wouldn't need it. She had left Con for a much richer man; his brother had more money than Con did, although they hadn't seemed quite sure where he had got it.

'Can't you give someone else instructions? Or don't you know yet what you want to keep?'

'I suppose I do,' Con said. 'Nothing, in fact—when I left, I took everything that mattered. What's left in the house doesn't mean a thing to me. I'd rather travel light from now on; I'm never accumulating a lot of things again. She's welcome to it all.' He was trying for a light tone, but only managed to sound very bitter, and Maddie felt even more sorry for him. She was careful not to show it, of course; he would hate that.

He halted again outside the radio station, high on the hill above the town, perched like a seagull's nest on the white cliff with the foam and blue sea far below it, although at this hour you rarely saw the view. Most nights when Maddie went to work she found herself staring out at blackness; tonight, though, the moon illuminated beach and sea almost as brightly as daylight.

'Why not ask your solicitor to go, then?' she suggested to Con, who stared down at her, shaking his head.

'Jill would think I was making a point, insulting her. She'll be there—even worse, she'll think I'm scared of seeing her.'

'Can't you plead pressure of work?'

He laughed. 'I always did—that was one reason for the break-up of our marriage. I worked too hard, I was never there.'

Perhaps he secretly wanted to go? thought Maddie, suppressing a smile. He was pretending he didn't want to see his wife, when in fact he did, badly.

Then Con said, 'Maddie, I hate to ask this . . .'

'Yes?' She smiled blithely, not expecting what came next.

'Would you go tomorrow?'

It was Maddie's turn to look utterly blank and stare, to repeat his words. 'Go? Tomorrow?'

'To the house,' Con said quickly, pleadingly. 'See my wife, explain that I can't make it, something urgent has come up and anyway I don't want anything, she can do as she likes with it all. Keep the lot herself, if she likes, or sell it. I'll leave the decision to her, she can't complain about that—although she will, you'll see. Whatever I do isn't good enough. Jill hates me. You would think it was me who had left her, instead of the other way around. The bitterness is all on her side.'

It didn't sound as if it was, thought Maddie, staring at him, dumbfounded. Was he serious? He couldn't really expect her to keep a rendezvous with his wife for him—or could he?

'Con, I really don't think this is a good idea,' she began, tentatively, but he did not let her finish.

'Frankly, I can't trust anyone else to go,' he said, taking her hand and looking very seriously at her. 'Our friends have split fifty-fifty; those on my side are dead against Jill, and those who've taken her side are dead against me. I don't want my solicitor to go because that makes it too official; Jill would resent that. And I can't ask a friend or even a relative in case whoever I send gets into a row with Jill.'

'Your secretary?' Maddie was grasping at straws, and saw his wry grin with a sinking heart.

'Enid? She's so much on my side, it's embarrassing, and Jill can't stand the sight of her, anyway.'

Maddie was not surprised to hear about Enid's partiality; it was well known in Seaborough Radio that Enid was half in love with her boss. Sighing, she looked at her watch and groaned.

'I must rush, Con—just look at the time!'

She turned to go and he caught her hand. 'Maddie, please? Will you go there for me?'

His helpless eyes were her undoing; she was defeated by her own sense of pity. Maddie hated to see people in pain or unhappy; she couldn't say no to him, however much she might distrust this scheme.

Con read the look on her face and sighed. 'Thanks, Maddie. I knew I could rely on you.'

It was only then that she wondered if he had had this at the back of his mind when he'd asked her to dinner. She had believed it to be her own idea, but had he been waiting for her to suggest it? Con was capable of it.

'I'll give you the address,' he said, producing a small

notebook and writing rapidly before tearing out a page. 'Here—you can't miss the house. The gates are blue, you'll see the name-plate from the bottom of the hill. Can you get there by eleven?'

'In the morning?' she asked, aghast. She was rarely up before noon because her show ran until two in the morning; she went home to bed immediately, but it was not easy to get to sleep after giving out on the air for two hours. Her adrenalin was still high and she was excited. She listened to soft music and read until she fell asleep, which was usually around four. To get to Con's old house by eleven she would have to be up and eating breakfast by ten.

'I'm sorry, can you manage?' Con asked contritely, and she shrugged. Six hours' sleep? Well, she had had less and it had not killed her.

'OK,' she said, and was given one of Con's sweet, brilliant smiles; they changed his whole face and made him irresistible to anyone exposed to them. Maddie found herself smiling back and yet wryly knew herself to have been bamboozled into doing just as he wanted. That was Con's technique; to charm people into acting against their own best interests. He got away with it because people still liked him even after they had realised how he had talked them round. He was quite right, too; people in this town took his side or that of his wife, and close friends of Con could be quite violent about Jill Osborne. Maddie had only been in Seaborough for six months, but she had already discovered how the divorce had split the Osbornes' friends in two camps.

She waved goodbye and walked across the foyer,

pausing to sign herself in at the desk under the friendly eye of the night porter, Mr Hobbs, one of the old school: upright, soldierly, a stickler for the rules.

'Thank you, miss,' he said, scrutinising her signature as if it might be forged. 'Nice night—get colder before dawn—no cloud cover.'

'And very bright moonlight,' she agreed, walking towards the lift, leaving Mr Hobbs looking out distrustfully at the moon.

Maddie was quite at home in a studio; she did not need an engineer to help her although, of course, there was one in the control room on night duty. Maddie worked the control panel herself; fading her discs up and down, operating an echo channel now and then for fun, her soft, husky voice whispering into the mike between music. She liked a certain sound, music for night listening: poignant, nostalgic, soothing. Luckily, her taste seemed to hit the button with her audience; her listening figures had grown steadily since she had started broadcasting with Seaborough. Con was very pleased with the response; not merely the size of the audience, but the letters and phone calls they received, too.

She had a lot of requests and played most of them; people asked for the sort of stuff she liked playing, they knew her taste well by now and seemed to share it. At that hour of the night you did not want pop music which blasted you out of the room, but some jazz or blues suited a night-time mood and Maddie played a lot of both, as well as pop classics and gentle ballads.

That night she got a few regulars; night-workers who often called and whose voices were already familiar to her.

'Hello, Maddie,' they said with cheerful intimacy, proud of having talked to her before. 'This is Fred,' or Annie or Pete, as the case might be; and she would ask, 'How are you tonight, Fred? Job going well?' Fine, they would say, just fine—or jokily tell her it was getting them down, so would she play an old favourite for them?

One voice was quite new—a deep, amused voice. 'Will you play "Smoke Gets in Your Eyes" for me?'

'Sure,' she said. 'Glad to, if I can find it, but for now will you tell us your name, stranger?'

'Stranger will do,' he said, and the sound of his voice sent shivers down her spine. It was that sort of voice, the vibrations of it intensely sexy. He could be an actor, she thought; he knew what his voice could do, anyway. It was trained.

'You don't live here, then?' she guessed, oddly curious about him.

'No, just passing through.'

'On holiday?'

'Visiting,' he admitted cagily. Usually people were eager to tell you all about themselves. If they rang you it was because they wanted to talk, often *needed* to talk. They couldn't wait to pour out the story of their lives on the air; sometimes they confessed painful secrets or sad stories, you had difficulty curtailing them, although Maddie had evolved a gentle technique by now—you had to if you were not to lose control of the show.

Why had this man rung? He seemed to have nothing to say, so perhaps he really did just want to hear that record?

'Well, Stranger——' she began, and he interrupted in that sexy voice.

'What do you look like, Maddie? I'm trying to imagine you.'

She sat upright, her smile vanishing. Oh, no, not one of those! You got them from time to time, the freaks who wanted to make sexual innuendo part of the show. She was disappointed; he had sounded so nice, and she had even been trying to guess what he looked like. She had felt oddly as if they were alone together in the night; it was easy to forget all the thousands of listening ears when you were alone in the studio, listening to another voice through the headphones.

'I'm afraid I can't get hold of your chosen record, Stranger, but I'll have it for you by tomorrow night, so tune in then at midnight through two a.m. to hear *Maddie's Midnight Music*, soft sounds for people who can't sleep or have to work. In the meantime, I hope you like this . . .'

Before he could say another word she had keyed him out and turned up the next disc, leaning back in her chair with one eye on the large clock just above the control panel. A light flashed on the panel and she picked up the in-house phone; the studio engineer was on the line.

'You seem to get one every night now,' he chuckled. 'There are a lot of love-maddened men out there listening to you, Maddie.'

'And he sounded rather nice, too,' she complained.

'Maybe it's the music you play; sexy stuff, jazz.'

She laughed. 'You think so?'

'Don't you? How about lunch tomorrow, by the way?'

'I'd have loved to, Jack, but I have an appointment tomorrow and I don't know when I'll be free. Can I take a rain check?'

'Friday?'

He was persistent, and Maddie did like him, so she agreed to meet him on Friday. When he had rung off she checked with the radio station operator to make sure that Stranger would not be put through if he rang again. That was standard procedure, but Maddie wanted to be quite certain he did not slip through the usual net.

'He isn't one of our regulars, is he?' asked the girl on switchboard. 'I thought he was just curious about you, he seemed genuine to me. After all, you're just a voice to them, unless they happen to see your picture in the local paper. It's only natural to wonder what you look like.' She giggled. 'Actually, I was rather wondering what *he* looked like. I loved his voice!'

So had Maddie, and she had been wondering what he looked like, too, so maybe she was over-reacting to his comment, but she wasn't going to take chances on the air. You had to be sure you weren't giving air-time to nutcases.

Next morning, she found an envelope from Con on her doormat when she struggled out of bed and started for the kitchen of her small flat. She was up earlier than usual and felt grim. While she drank some strong coffee and ate a slice of toast and marmalade, she read through the note Con had dropped through her letterbox while she slept. He kept early hours, usually at his desk by half-past eight, so he must have called in on his way to work. He had put the front-door key of his old home into the envelope, and she weighed it in her palm, staring at it.

It was a sad little object, all that was left of a marriage. Maddie shivered. Poor Con, she didn't blame him for feeling unable to face his wife, but it was not going to be too pleasant for her, either. Con's instructions were crystal-clear and should be easy to carry through, however. Jill Osborne wouldn't have anything to complain about. Con was being ultra-generous.

It was a clear, bright morning in early spring; the trees greening and a few primroses already out in the hedges lining the country road along which Maddie had to drive out of Seaborough to reach Con's old home. She had trouble keeping her eyes on the road; the landscape kept luring her gaze aside. The earth was a rich reddish loam, the grass very green, the sky cloudless and the hills warmly rolling in an endless line of folds from the coast as far as the eye could follow.

Con had told her how to find the house; he had said it would be easy, and he was right. Within twenty minutes she was driving up a banked hill, through the blue gates, parking in front of the charming white house. She sat behind the wheel and stared up at it. Con had said it had been empty since he and his wife had left, but it did not have that blank look which empty houses soon seem to get. It was a warm, welcoming family house and Maddie loved it on sight. It must have been quite a wrench for Con to leave it and move into a flat in Seaborough, but it would probably have been even more painful to stay on, alone, with all those memories.

There was no sign of another car, so perhaps Jill Osborne wasn't here yet. Should she wait? Or let herself into the house with the key Con had provided?

She looked at her watch and decided to wait another five minutes; it was only just eleven, now. Con's wife might arrive any minute.

Ten minutes later there was still no sign of Jill Osborne and Maddie was bored, sitting in the car listening to the radio, so she got out and walked around the house, glancing in at all the windows without seeing a soul. It was brisk and chilly out there, she might as well wait in the house as she had to pick up two books which Con had overlooked in his study when he'd cleared out all his papers, records and books the day he'd moved into town.

She let herself into the house and walked across the hall to the apple-green-papered little study; the bookshelves almost denuded of books, the record cabinets open and empty, the leather-topped desk bare. The room had a sad feeling. Maddie picked up the two books which still stood on the shelves, and turned to go. Maybe Con's wife had changed her mind, too? Maybe she wasn't coming, either?

It was then that she heard the faint creak of a floorboard upstairs. She froze, listening, a frown between her brows. Had she imagined that? No, there it was again; someone was moving about upstairs.

Maddie walked quickly out into the hall to the foot of the wide oak-tread stairs.

'Mrs Osborne?' she called, her head back and her

grey eyes fixed on the landing above.

A door opened. She watched the change of the light, a brightening and then a shadow on the pale blue walls as someone walked along the landing. It wasn't a woman, it was a man, a very tall man whose shadow elongated upwards over the ceiling, making her draw a sharp breath of alarm for some reason.

He stood on the top stair, eyeing her, and Maddie asked huskily, 'Who are you?'

He didn't answer, and the hairs stood up on the back of her neck. Before she actually saw him, she had thought he might be the local auctioneer, who was to handle the sale of the house, but she knew Richard Lucas quite well, and this was not him. Of course, he might work for Richard.

'Do you work for Lucas's?' she asked, sounding nervous, and furious with herself for doing so.

'Do I look as if I do?' he asked, and the sound of his voice sent shock-waves through her. She stood there, staring; he certainly didn't look as if he worked for Richard Lucas, although he was casually dressed in a loose, black fisherman's sweater and old black cord trousers. In spite of the casual clothes, his air wasn't that of a workman. He was far too sure of himself; his blue eyes held a glint of cool intelligence, as if he knew everything about her. He made Maddie's skin burn with awareness, and that made her angrier.

'Who are you?' she asked again, stupidly, but convinced that she had heard that voice before. It had an unforgettable timbre.

'Hello, Maddie,' he said, and her pulses leapt and raced.

CHAPTER TWO

MADDIE had never seen him before in her life, but she knew that voice. Last night she had been sure she would recognise it again if she ever heard it, and she had been right. She did.

'I don't know you,' she said, though, warily moving backwards in case she needed to make a run for it.

'Don't you, Maddie?' he mocked, coming down the stairs.

'How do you know who I am?' He hadn't even hesitated. How on earth had he known?

'Doesn't everybody around here know you?'

It was true; in Seaborough she had rapidly become a household name. This was a small town, and the radio was an important part of local life. All the same, she didn't relax. His shadow had exaggerated his height, but he was still a very tall man and he made her nervous.

'What are you doing in this house?' she attacked, head up. Had he followed her here? But how had he got in?

'I was looking around upstairs while I waited.' He was on the same level now, but that only made him seem taller.

'You didn't answer my question!'

'Which one?'

'Don't be tricky,' Maddie snapped, watching him suspiciously. She had only heard his voice for a moment last night on the air, but somehow it already seemed intensely familiar. She had wondered if *he* was as attractive as his voice, and couldn't help staring. He was, she couldn't deny it—tall, dark and casually, confidently attractive. A man who had no qualms about his looks and identity, utterly self-assured. Maddie found that infuriating even as she envied it. She didn't feel that sure of herself.

'Who are you and how did you get in here?' she insisted.

'I used a key,' he drawled, dangling a key ring from one hand.

'Who gave you that?' Maddie asked, taken aback. 'The house agent? The house isn't on the market yet. He had no right to give you a key and let you wander around on your own.'

'Jill Osborne gave it to me.'

'Con's wife?' Maddie flushed; could he be the man she had left Con for? His brother? Her eyes hunted over him for evidence of a resemblance, but there was none. He and Con were miles apart in every way: colouring, build, height, bone structure.

'Is Mrs Osborne here?' she stammered, glancing up the stairs.

'No,' he said. 'She didn't come.'

'She hasn't come?' Maddie couldn't believe it—after all Con's agonising, his wife simply hadn't bothered to turn up?

'There seemed to be no point . . .'

'No point?' Maddie interrupted, flushed with anger. 'No point in coming back this once to decide what should happen to their home? They *were* married, this is all that's left of that—she might have had the decency to come back to make a civilised settlement about all the things they shared.'

His dark brows had risen sharply. 'You seem very angry about something that's hardly your business.' His eyes narrowed. 'Or is it?'

'What?' Maddie was too angry to get his drift. 'What are you talking about?'

'Con Osborne—*is* he your business?'

She got the point then, her whole body hot with outrage at what he was implying.

'No, he is not! He's my boss, that's all, and I like him. I also think it isn't much to ask for Jill Osborne to be here today to settle what's to happen to the home she and Con shared.'

'So where's he, then?' drawled the other, and Maddie's teeth met. She might have known that he would put a sure finger on the weakness in her argument, but it wasn't fair to Con—he wasn't here for very different reasons from his wife's. Jill hadn't bothered to come because she apparently didn't see the point of turning up. It meant nothing at all to her. Con, on the other hand, cared *too* much.

'He would have come,' she excused defiantly. 'But . . .'

'But something more important came up at work?' he finished for her, his mouth wry. 'Yes, the same old excuse—that was what destroyed the marriage in the first place. He was always too busy at work to have time for her, and when his solicitor rang Jill to tell her that Con wouldn't be here today, she saw no point in coming herself. She asked me to deal with it.'

Maddie looked hard at him. 'Why you?' Her glance ran over him from head to toe, her expression dismissive. 'You don't look like a solicitor to me.'

'I'm glad about that, because I'm not one,' he murmured.

'Then who are you? How do I know you really are acting for Mrs Osborne?' *Was* he Con's brother?

'Your voice is very misleading,' he complained, strolling closer, and Maddie tried to back further, only to find herself up against the solid oak door. She lifted her chin and eyed him coldly.

'Answer my question!'

'On the air last night I thought you had one of the sexiest voices I've ever heard, and from the picture of you in the local paper's list of radio programmes I decided your face matched your voice.'

Her face flowed with startled colour and her eyes opened wide, the pupils dilated. She heard him laugh softly, amused by her unnerved reaction. Maddie was furious with herself; she was used to men making passes. It had certainly happened often enough since she'd started working in radio. It was one of the hazards of the job. Your voice went out over the air and into people's homes, and total strangers began to believe they knew you intimately. Lonely people began fantasising about you—occasionally a man convinced himself it was mutual, you felt the same about him.

Maddie's mail was sometimes very odd indeed; it was one part of the job she found a little disturbing, although so far she had always coped with it. Maddie was tough, she often told herself so; she could take the rough with the smooth.

Why, then, did this man get to her? He had, she couldn't deny it, right from the start. On the phone last night that voice of his had made the hair stand up on the back of her neck. She had panicked then, on the air, cut him off because she couldn't handle it, and she knew she couldn't handle it now, when he was actually there, in the flesh, and that phrase conjured up images that made her feel even more nervy.

'Don't you ever smile?' he murmured, and to her shock she felt his finger brush her mouth; a featherlight touch that sent heat rushing through her whole body.

'Don't!' she gasped, jerking her head away as if the touch had been an unbearable intrusion. He stared down at her, his brows rising.

'Well, well,' he drawled, smiling. 'Who'd have thought it?'

'Who'd have thought what?' She was answering like an automaton, but her mind was elsewhere, trying to understand why she had reacted like that, with such over-the-top violence, to a mere gesture.

'And I had you down as the sophisticated kind,' he murmured, looking so amused she could have hit him.

'As you've only just met me, I don't see how you

could have me down as anything at all!' she snapped, eyeing him with dislike. Why was he smiling like that?

'It must be your job,' he said. 'It had me fooled, I suppose. The kind of music you like, your voice, what you said on the air last night—it all added up to a certain image.'

'I've heard that before,' Maddie said scornfully. 'From men on the make. Well, I'm not available, and if you make another pass at me I'll smack your face.'

He laughed, blue eyes teasing, inviting her to find that funny, too—the very idea of her hitting him and getting away with it. He towered over her, lean though he was, a casually powerful man in those casual clothes—and that was the keynote of his attitude, the casual approach. This man didn't try to impress or insist, he was coolly laid-back and sure of himself. Too damned clever by half, thought Maddie, meeting the blue gleam of his glance. She would have to watch him, be wary of him. For some reason she couldn't yet work out, he worried her. He wasn't threatening, yet she felt threatened. Her nerves were jumping like fire-crackers! And what made it far worse was that he *knew*.

She didn't know *how,* or precisely *what* he knew, but although they had certainly never met before she felt as if they had known each other for a long time. Looking into his eyes she read an amused awareness of her—even of what she was thinking now. He could read her mind. She almost felt that he was ahead of her, could guess what she would think, and, scariest of all, Maddie felt the same instant, disturbed awareness of him, the same troubling familiarity.

She had felt it last night at the first sound of his voice, she felt it increasingly with every minute that she spent in his company, and it bothered her. She was as jumpy as a cat on hot bricks, and she wanted to get away from him.

'Well, as Mrs Osborne isn't coming, I see no point in hanging around here,' she said, her voice husky. 'I'm going.'

'You're not,' he said smoothly, moving before she could. A second later she was neatly caged inside his outstretched arms, his hands planted one on each side of her as he leaned on the wall. To get away she would have to make a fight of it, and they both knew she wouldn't do that—it would make this far too important.

She eyed him derisively. 'Stop playing games, Mr . . .? You haven't even told me your name.'

'Nash,' he said.

'I'm in no mood for this sort of thing, Mr Nash,' Maddie said, registering that he couldn't, after all, be Con's brother, the man Jill Osborne had run away with, and stupidly relieved about that, although why should it matter to her? He was just a stranger. Wasn't he?

'What are you in a mood for?' he asked, as if really intrigued, but she saw the faint twist of his mouth, the almost imperceptible rise of one brow, and knew that he was still teasing her.

'I thought you could read my mind,' she mocked

in her turn, and his mouth curled with amusement.

'But you're a woman, after all—and that makes you unfathomable at times.'

'I'm glad to hear it,' she said, with more insistence than was wise.

'I'm sure you are,' he drawled, staring into her eyes.

Maddie struggled to look unflustered, but knew that her colour was rising even higher. To distract him from the personal conflict between them, she attacked on another front. 'Why did Jill Osborne send *you* today?'

He shrugged. 'She would have felt humiliated if she had come herself, since Con had backed out. In any case, she doesn't want anything from the house—Con can have whatever he wants, and sell the rest, she says.'

Maddie was startled. She had imagined that Con's wife would want some of the antique furniture, which was clearly very valuable. Con had told her that it had been Jill who had chosen the furniture. Jill, he said, was passionately fond of old furniture, and had taken great pleasure in choosing pieces for their home, haunting auction rooms and antique shops to find exactly what she wanted. Why didn't she want any of these beautiful things? Maddie was no expert, but she had seen several things she would love to own.

'But . . .' she began, and stopped. He looked enquiringly at her, one brow lifted.

'Yes?'

Maddie hesitated, then broke out raggedly, 'Con

told me to say he didn't want anything, either! Why was this meeting arranged at all—if neither of them wanted to come and neither of them wanted anything from the house?'

He shrugged. 'The lawyers dreamt it up, I imagine—a safeguard for their clients, for both of them to be present when the auctioneer went round the house and assessed the contents. Then both parties to the divorce would be able to check that nothing had been removed before the sale.'

It made sense, and Maddie sighed. 'Yes, I suppose that must be it.' She looked at her watch and at the same moment heard the note of a car engine in the driveway. Her stomach turned over with relief. That must be the auctioneer arriving at last! She didn't know how much longer she could have borne being alone with Mr Nash.

Her smoky grey eyes lifted to his face briefly and caught the dry amusement in his stare again.'

'Feel braver now, do you?' he mocked.

'You're a mind-reader,' she retorted and he laughed.

'I don't need to be with you. Your face is very expressive.'

'What's it expressing now?' she asked, staring back at him with unmasked hostility. She didn't like feeling so edgy and that was how this man made her feel, so she did not like him.

The doorbell chimed and she jumped. Mr Nash didn't bother to answer her last question; he moved away and Maddie turned to open the front door.

'Mrs Osborne . . .' began Richard Lucas and

then stopped, staring. 'Oh, hello, Maddie—you here with Con?'

'I'm here *instead* of Con, Richard.'

Richard thoughtfully smoothed back a perfectly tidy strand of silvery hair. He was only in his thirties, but his dark hair had already turned a very becoming silver which made his thin face seem far more attractive and amazingly young. He was a good-looking man, and would have been even better looking if he hadn't been so aware of his looks. He was like an actor, always conscious of himself and how he was behaving. He moved gracefully, calm and considered in every gesture and movement. He dressed elegantly: pin-striped suits made by the best tailor in town, expensive shirts and ties, handmade shoes, because he had very small, very thin feet, and couldn't find ready-made shoes to fit them.

Maddie liked him, but he made her want to smile. He was just too perfect; it wasn't bearable.

'And Jill . . .?' he enquired, and she gestured at Mr Nash.

Richard looked amazed; his eyes opened very wide and his mouth opened too, although he didn't say anything.

'Shut your mouth, Richard,' Mr Nash advised gently, and Richard went a little red with resentment because he hated knowing that he had been betrayed into an unconsidered response. It lacked dignity, and Richard took his dignity seriously, very seriously indeed.

Maddie would have enjoyed this by-play rather more if she had not been so puzzled by it. Richard obviously knew Mr Nash, and Mr Nash equally obviously knew him well, too. Richard had been very surprised to see him, though—he certainly had not been expecting him.

Which again raised the question—who exactly was Mr Nash? And how did he come to be here, standing in for Jill Osborne? Maddie had never seen him before, which meant that almost certainly he did not live in Seaborough or she would have done. The town was small and she had met most of the well known inhabitants or, at the very least, heard their names or read them in the local paper. Yet, if he didn't live here, how did Richard know him?

Was he related to Jill Osborne? Her brother, perhaps? Or was he a relative of Con's who did not actually live in Seaborough but had visited it?

'Hello, Zachary,' Richard was saying, shaking hands. He was very stiff; you couldn't say he was overwhelmed with delight at seeing Mr Nash again.

Zachary? thought Maddie. The name seemed vaguely familiar, but that wasn't why she was turning it over and over in her mind. Did it suit him? she was thinking, staring. Zachary. It was unusual, you couldn't deny that, and if you had to be called Zachary it probably helped to look the way he did. You would need quite a bit of confidence to carry it off!

'How are you?' Richard asked, always polite.

'Fine, thanks—and you?'

They were so formal, but then men were, in a difficult situation, especially when they did not like each other too much, anyway. Maddie watched them wryly. They were really quite funny, although she knew they wouldn't laugh if *she* did; they didn't see each other from the same angle or themselves from outside, the way she did.

Richard cleared his throat and looked portentous. 'Well,' he said, to show that the first courtesy was over. 'Shall we get on? What exactly is the position about the contents of the house, then?'

'Everything goes,' Zachary Nash said succinctly, and Maddie winced.

It was true, but it was a brutal way of putting it. Poor Con, this was going to be tough on him. Maddie was sure he still loved his wife; she had seen it in his eyes last night, he hadn't really tried to hide it. Con was badly hurt and he was going to hate the idea of strangers invading his old home, wandering around the rooms which had once been the private centre of his whole world, touching his possessions, bargaining over them. It would strip his personal dignity to the bone. No wonder he hadn't been able to come today!

Richard was looking at her, a question in his face. 'Maddie?'

Her grey eyes misty with anger and the memory of Con's pain, she took a deep breath and then nodded.

'Everything?' repeated Richard, surprised. 'Con doesn't want to keep anything at all? Are you sure?'

'It's all to be sold,' Maddie said, as Con had told her to, but she couldn't help wondering if Con really meant it. Wasn't he going to regret this one day—maybe very soon? She had the strong feeling that Con was acting emotionally, in bitterness, rather than with common sense.

Richard shrugged, however, used to the vagaries of clients, no doubt, and a little cynical about them. It was just business to him; why should it be anything else?

'Very well. We'll make a start on the top floor and work our way downwards, shall we?'

'When is the auction?' Maddie asked.

'We haven't fixed a date yet, but probably next month.'

At least it gave Con time to change his mind, Maddie thought, as she and Zachary followed Richard around the house. However, she was increasingly depressed as time dragged on—she had never realised how many *things* a house could hold. Richard was conscientiously intent on recording every single one of them—from antique chairs to a shabby Persian carpet and even an old broom in the kitchen. He stuck circles of white paper on each item, bearing a lot number. The rash spread throughout the house—everything bore a white spot, everything was doomed. Con's house was about to break up, to disperse for ever.

It was very sad and Maddie had had enough, she wanted to get away. She kept looking at her watch and sighing, and in the end even Richard had to take note of her impatience.

'Getting tired, Maddie?'

'And hungry,' she said. 'And bored. I want my lunch—don't you?'

'Well, we could start again this afternoon,'

Richard said reluctantly.

'Not me,' said Maddie. 'I've got better things to do. Con can come this afternoon, if he likes, but I have had it.' She walked away, a slim girl in a pleated blue skirt and white sweater, moving well, sure of herself, her sleek black head up and her eyes direct, bright with irritation.

'There's a good restaurant down the hill,' Zachary Nash said at her back and she turned her head without halting.

'I'm driving back to town, I'll eat there.'

'Lunch will be over long before you get there, but if we hurry we can just make lunch at this place down the hill.'

Maddie unlocked her car without answering, got behind the wheel and turned to say coldly that she did not want to have lunch with him. He wasn't there. Surprised, she began to look about for him, and found him just getting into the front passenger seat next to her.

'What are you doing?' she asked, startled, scowling.

'Putting on my seat-belt,' he said, deftly clipping the metal buckle into place.

'Now, look——' said Maddie, teeth tight.

'Hurry up or we'll be too late for lunch, and you'll kick yourself for missing one of the best meals you'll ever eat. They have a first-class chef—his navarin of lamb is out of this world.'

'I'm eating in town. Will you get out of my car? Where's yours?' She looked around, remembering that she hadn't seen a car parked here when she arrived.

'I haven't got one—I came on foot.'

She stared, eyes rounding. 'Walked? Where from?'

'This hotel down the hill,' he drawled, and the penny dropped.

'The one with the fantastic chef?'

'The very same,' he admitted, laughing.

'I suppose I should have guessed. And you want a lift back?' She started the car and drove out of the gate, her mouth wry. 'Why didn't you just say so? There's no need to bribe me just to get a lift.'

'Bribe you?'

She looked sideways and saw his profile: a hard edge of bone and flesh, amazingly elegant in line, lashes covering his eyes and a glint of brilliance showing through them. He was still mocking her; Maddie felt like hitting him.

'With lunch,' she snapped.

'I *want* to buy you lunch,' he murmured, shifting, and his leg brushed hers. She had the weirdest sensation she had ever had in her life. The car swerved, tyres skidding.

'Hey!' he said, sitting up.

'Sorry, a patch of frost on the road,' she lied huskily, getting back on course and gripping the steering wheel tightly between both hands. My God! what had happened to her then? A peculiar sinking feeling in the pit of her stomach, as if she had suddenly fallen from a cliff or the roof of a building, rushing downwards at speed, her whole body disorientated—what did it mean?

Nothing important, she told herself hurriedly. High blood pressure, or low blood sugar, lack of sleep or lack of food—you could blame it on anything you liked, but one thing it certainly was not—it had nothing whatever to do with Zachary Nash.

He had not made her pulses leap and roar, or her stomach sink down through the floor. Not on your life! He hadn't and he never would.

'Turn left,' he said, and the sound of his voice made her jump again, swallowing hard.

Maddie was so busy thinking about how much she never thought about him that she obeyed implicitly, and a moment later had pulled up outside a large hotel. It had obviously been converted from a country house; it had an absent-minded, gracious air, like a surprised hostess who can't remember inviting you to her party. The Regency façade had been carefully preserved; good proportions, like good bone structure, are essential for beauty. The windows, portico, roof and doors made a harmonious whole, and the house was set among green lawns dominated by a vast, tranquil cedar, the fans of dark green branches sweeping the grass on all sides and making a shadowy tent below.

'I seem to be the only guest,' Zachary Nash told her drily, unclipping his seat-belt. 'Apart from Jill, anyway.'

'Mrs Osborne?' Maddie gave him an incredulous, startled look. 'She's staying here?'

'She was. She said she was leaving today, but I don't know if she meant it.'

'Is she here alone?'

He nodded and Maddie frowned—presumably Con's brother had not felt he could face Con, and he was probably wise to stay away. Maddie hadn't heard much about him, except that he had inherited a fortune from an uncle and lived in London. He and Con had never been on good terms, she had gathered, there was rivalry between them long ago, before Jill Osborne married Con. She had just been a weapon in the feud between the brothers, perhaps? Had she walked out on her lover when she realised she had been used?

'Have you known her long?' she asked Zachary Nash, who was getting out of the car.

He walked round to her side before answering. 'Since she was in nappies,' he said smiling, leaning in the window.

Maddie was too interested in the subject of Jill Osborne to guess what he meant to do—one minute she was staring intently at his lean, dark face, and the next she was stiffening in affront as she saw him snatch her ignition key.

'What are you . . .'

'Out you get,' he said coolly, opening her door.

'Give me back my keys!' She stayed where she was, hand outstretched.

'Come and get them,' he said with that familiar, infuriating amusement, strolling away.

'Come back here!' Maddie yelled at his back, but he didn't look round or pause; he disappeared into the hotel and she had no option but to go after him.

She caught up with him in the hotel lobby.

Maddie stopped in her tracks as she saw who he was talking to—a tall girl in a chic, tailor-made cream dress. One look, and Maddie guessed her identity. It had to be Jill Osborne.

Slender, beautiful, her manner coolly poised and her long, dark hair swept up into a chignon, there was no doubt in Maddie's mind at all. 'Looks like a model,' someone had once told her of Jill. 'Classy, legs up to here!' People had described Jill in detail many times.

They hadn't talked about Jill's family at all that Maddie could recall. They hadn't said that she had a brother, but, seeing her next to Zachary Nash now, Maddie wondered if they were related. They had the same colouring, the same assurance, they were talking with an easy familiarity which was affectionate and intimate, without being in any way sexual. They talked like brother and sister, or old friends, not at all like lovers.

But, if they were related, why hadn't he said so? Did he dislike being asked personal questions? Maddie knew some people did. Or had it just been one of his deliberate teases? The man liked playing games, she knew that already. It might have amused him to mystify her, withhold betraying bits of information.

What were they talking about? Their heads were close together, their faces intent. Con? Or her?

Zachary suddenly looked round, and then so did Jill, with the same gesture, the same turn of the head. There was the same look on their faces—shuttered, secretive, excluding her from whatever they had been saying, or were thinking now. They had closed ranks. She, after all, was an outsider, not one of the family. She sensed that they wouldn't talk openly in front of her, but she couldn't help wondering what they had been saying.

Zachary put a hand under Jill's elbow, and they walked towards Maddie.

She was oddly nervous; why she should be she could not say, but she definitely was and felt her flush deepening.

'Jill, this is Madeleine Ferrall—Maddie, this is Jill.'

Jill Osborne's hand was slim and cool, like Jill herself. Shaking hands, Maddie was conscious of being shorter, less graceful, far less elegantly dressed. Jill reminded her of her own sister, Penny; old feelings swamped her for a second, a feeling of inferiority and uncertainty, the nightmares of adolescence rising up again.

Then Jill smiled and said, 'I've heard you on the air, and I did enjoy your show. You're so witty—I could never talk so casually and be so funny—it comes naturally to you, I suppose, but I must say I envy you the gift.'

'Of the gab? Thanks,' Maddie said, laughing and relaxing. 'At school, it got me into trouble all the time.'

'I just bet it did,' said Zachary Nash, but she ignored him.

'Answering back, they called it at school.'

'That's what I'd call it now,' said Zachary.

'I'm not talking to you,' Maddie told him without looking in his direction. 'And you can give me back my car key right now.'

'I thought you weren't talking to me?'

'Just give it back and I'll be on my way!' she told him, her hand outstretched.

He considered it thoughtfully, his head to one side. 'Do you bite your nails?'

Maddie snatched her hand away, very red. She had tried to cure herself of the habit for years; sometimes she seemed to have stopped for good, but whenever tension built up inside her she started again. She hadn't noticed herself chewing her nails lately, though; she must have done it without realising what she was doing.

'Give me my car key, damn you, you . . .' Whatever adjective she had been about to apply to him died in her throat as she remembered Jill Osborne's presence and looked her way, biting her lip.

Jill was looking surprised and Maddie gave her a forced smile. 'Is he always like this?'

'Yes,' said Jill, laughing.

'Like what?' he enquired with pleased interest; like most men, he seemed to love being talked about by women.

'I haven't got the time to tell you, it would take all day,' Maddie informed him, her hand peremptorily held out. 'Now, give me my car key!'

'Come and have lunch,' was all he said, turning away. 'You're obviously hungry; your blood sugar is probably low, that's what's making you so edgy.'

'It isn't my blood sugar making me bad-tempered—it's you!' she told him through her teeth.

She kept up with him, grabbing his arm, and Jill Osborne murmured in a surprised tone, 'Zach, really! What are you doing?'

He stopped and looked round at her; Maddie saw their eyes meet in silent understanding. Zachary Nash dug deep into his trouser pocket and found Maddie's key; he tossed it to her, shrugging.

'Thank you,' she said, but didn't leave at once. She turned to Jill and began politely, 'It was nice to meet you . . .' but then could not think of anything more to add because Jill had hurt Con so badly, and Maddie admired Con and liked him very much. Con had been so right when he said that people had to choose; you couldn't be on both sides of the fence when a marriage broke up. The pair involved wouldn't let you; you were either with them or against them, and Maddie was with Con, she cared about him. It would hurt him if he knew that she had made friends with his ex-wife, he would feel betrayed. He had asked her to come today because she was on his side, she had never known his wife, she couldn't be disloyal.

She sighed and smiled, then turned to go. She had known last night that she should not agree to come in Con's place; it had instinctively seemed an unwise thing to do and she had been quite right.

She wished she hadn't come, hadn't met Zachary Nash and Jill, hadn't seen the other side of the fence, the alternative version of the story behind the divorce. She didn't know why Jill had left Con, of course, she hadn't discussed anything personal with her, yet she knew her now and she sensed that there was more to it than people had said. It wasn't as simple as they had made it seem—what ever was?

People liked to simplify things, make them easier to grasp or swallow, they ignored the bits that didn't fit their easy explanation. She must have been simple-minded herself to believe them; life wasn't a matter of black or white, good or bad, wrong or right. Life was half-tones, greys, the music between the notes; it was never simple or easy. Now that she had met Jill, she found herself liking her, and questioning her own earlier, unthinking loyalty to Con, and Maddie was disturbed by that.

She did not want her life complicated by being cut up by a quarrel which was really not her business. If she stayed here and got to know Jill better, she would find herself being drawn deeper into this abyss between the two of them. It was safer and easier to stay on Con's side.

'Sorry, I have to go,' she said over her shoulder, hurrying away, relieved when Zachary Nash made no attempt to follow.

It wasn't Zachary who caught up with her in the car park, it was Jill, and Maddie looked round at her in wary surprise.

Jill gave her a quivery smile, her lips unsteady. 'I just wanted to . . .' Her voice was husky and then broke; she took a deep breath and forced it out. 'How's Con?'

Maddie felt as if she had been kicked in the stomach. The naked pain in the question made her gasp. It changed everything; she saw the situation from a totally new angle, and for a moment she could not even speak.

CHAPTER THREE

CON rang that evening, surprising Maddie in the shower. She ran for the phone, hurriedly winding herself into a bath towel, but still wet and dripping.

'Maddie?' The voice was immediately recognisable, although it wasn't as distinctive as Zachary's; the timbre not as deep nor as innately sexy. Con was businesslike; he talked rapidly, clipping off his words as if he did not have the time to finish them.

'Oh, hello, Con.' She spoke breathlessly, frowning—had some emergency come up? She was getting ready to leave for the studio and in a hurry. Con would know that—had he rung on business?

'What happened this morning? You didn't ring me,' he said, and only then did Maddie realise why he had rung. It wasn't that she had forgotten the events of the morning; they had been on her mind most of the day, but while she showered she had been thinking about work exclusively, everything else had been pushed out of her head.

'I'm sorry, I tried, but you weren't there and I didn't want to leave a message in case you wanted it kept private. Your wife didn't come, either, Con—she sent . . .'

'She didn't come?' he broke in, his tone harsh.

'No, she sent . . .'

'My God! She couldn't even be bothered to turn up?' Con was at once violently angry, which was not very logical, since he had not gone himself, but then you couldn't expect logic from a man in an emotional turmoil, thought Maddie.

'She didn't want anything from the house, either,' she said, intending to go on to tell him that she had actually met his wife in the end, but Con did not give her the chance.

'What?' he snarled, and Maddie held the phone away from her ear, wincing.

'Con, listen . . .'

'She didn't want *anything?*'

Neither had he, but that small fact seemed to have escaped his memory.

'She just threw it all back in my face?'

'Well, I wouldn't say that,' protested Maddie.

'I made a generous gesture, and she couldn't even be bothered to accept it?'

'Con, I think . . .'

'She hates me,' Con said hoarsely. 'She'd do anything to hurt me. I'm sorry I asked you to go, Maddie. I shouldn't have involved you.'

'Look, Con . . .' said Maddie, appalled.

There was a crash at the other end and she jumped. Con had hung up. Biting her lip, she replaced her own phone and stood there, dripping on the carpet, worrying about him.

He had jumped to all the wrong conclusions, he hadn't let her explain anything. Con was in the grip of strong emotion and his thinking was haywire, but then both he and his wife seemed to be acting like idiots. Maddie found it hard to credit that two apparently sane, intelligent people could make such fundamental mistakes in dealing with each other. Why were they behaving like this?

It had been obvious that Jill still cared about Con—she hadn't been acting when she'd asked in that raw way, 'How's Con?' Nobody could fake that look; it mirrored the one in Con's face whenever he talked about his wife. So why had she left him, feeling that way about him? And why didn't she go back?

Con cared, no question about it—surely Jill must know that? She hadn't been sure what to tell Jill; Con would not thank her for betraying his feelings to his wife but, on the other hand, how could she help if she didn't drop a few hints?

'He isn't very happy,' she had said gently, and Jill's face had tightened, her eyes brilliant with unshed tears.

'Isn't he?' She had sounded bitter, then. 'Then why didn't he come today? Why ring and cancel? He obviously didn't want to see me.'

'No, you're wrong, it isn't that,' Maddie had hurriedly told her. 'But he couldn't face it, you see.' Surely she could tell Jill that much, that Con had backed out because he was afraid of getting hurt by seeing Jill and knowing it was all over, final, finished.

'Oh, I *see!*' Jill had said. 'Typical of him—walking out on a situation he couldn't handle.'

Maddie had smiled wryly at her. 'That's men for you!'

'Why should we put up with it?' Jill had demanded, and Maddie hadn't been able to think of an answer to that. Jill was talking with tight lips, her voice thin and sharp with pain. 'If he really cared, he would have been there. We haven't seen each other for months, but he couldn't even be bothered to meet me this once. Too busy, he said, that's what he told my solicitor—pressure of work. How many times have I heard that? Too busy to take me out to a dinner party fixed up weeks before? Too busy to take me on holiday as arranged? Cancelled weekends, lunches . . . even on our wedding anniversary he didn't get there on time! We had booked dinner at a very special place and Con arrived an hour later. I sat there looking ridiculous and getting more and more angry, and then he said, "Why are you making so much fuss? I couldn't help it, this was an *important* business matter."'

Maddie had just stood there with the torrent of angry words pouring over her head, not daring to interrupt or try to stem it, flushed with embarrassment and compassion.

'Business was important, you notice! But not me. I wasn't important. Married a year, and he left me sitting there for an hour because something more important had come up.' Jill bit off the last word and stood there, fighting with tears. 'That was when I realised our marriage was no marriage,' she said. 'I was a sideshow in Con's life, a trivial entertainment he could take or leave. I didn't matter.'

'You do! I'm sure you do!' Maddie had said quickly, then, but Jill had shaken her head.

'No, you're wrong—and, anyway, it's too late now.' Then she had walked away.

Maddie walked slowly back to the bathroom now,

thinking about that—why was it too late now?

She had been thinking about this purely from the point of view of the husband and wife; Con and Jill so obviously still cared about each other, and it seemed crazy for them to part when they had so much going for them. But what about the third angle of the triangle? Con's brother, the man who had taken Jill away to London—where did he fit into all this? Jill didn't love him—how could she when she still loved Con?

Why had she gone away with Con's brother, though? It seemed an insane act; she must have known Con would find it unforgivable, any man would. Not only had Jill wrecked her marriage, she had wrecked Con's family—divided brother and brother for ever.

Did Con's brother love Jill? Maddie dried herself slowly and got dressed, preoccupied with all the question marks which thronged her mind. The whole situation was confused; people had acted in a way she found hard to understand, but then she was still very much an outsider, a stranger to this little town and the people who lived here. What did she know about Con and his family? Or about Jill?

The people of Seaborough loved to gossip, especially about Con Osborne, but Maddie had tried hard not to listen; she had not wanted to encourage all that talk. She hadn't been able to stop her ears, of course, and some talk had got through to her, but it had been haphazard, a strand of information here, a thread of scandal there. She knew some things, not others, and she wouldn't *ask*. She had picked up an entirely false impression of Jill Osborne, and in adjusting that image she found all the rest of her ideas about the break-up of Con's marriage shuffling around, changing pattern, becoming something quite different.

What was the real situation between Jill Osborne and Con's brother? Was he here in town with her? Were they living together? Was she planning to marry him once her divorce was final? Did he know she still loved Con? What sort of man was he?

Maddie had a lot of questions but no answers, and she knew she wouldn't ever ask anyone, because it really was not her business. She couldn't help wondering, but she would not get involved.

When she got to the radio station that evening she found a pile of letters waiting for her; that was her first job of the shift, reading through her mail, deciding which requests to play on the programme. Sometimes people asked for a record that she had played very recently; sometimes they asked for one she couldn't find in the record library, for they didn't keep very old records, it was largely modern stuff. Maddie sorted out letters that should be answered, discarded some that should be ignored—there were always a few, often obscene, always distasteful.

Two hours later she went out for a supper break, having set up her discs and done a quick run-through to make sure music and chat were exactly balanced and fitted the time.

Her show might look haphazard—in fact, it was *meant* to sound casual and improvised—but of course it was nothing of the kind. That would have been too risky. She timed all the discs to the second; knew exactly how long she had to talk between each one, and had a shorthand note of what she was planning to talk about. That part of the show was genuinely spontaneous—she didn't read from a script, but she always kept within the timing limits of the programme as a whole.

She was always afraid of either drying up on the air, or over-running her time. Balance was essential; you had to achieve it to end up with a good show.

When she took phone calls on the air she had to be doubly alert. Callers tended to talk too much or say things they shouldn't. Maddie needed the tact of an angel. In a real emergency she just flicked the key that cut them off; as she had with Zachary Nash. It was rare for a man to ring up and try to proposition her on the air, because the switchboard took their home number before they would accept them for the show. A caller was always asked to ring off and wait for the switchboard to ring them—it was a safety precaution in more ways than one and weeded out the weirdos, but it didn't always work. The occasional nutcase got through to her, but Maddie could deal with that; so far it had never worried her, she kept her cool and coped with whatever happened.

At night, the canteen only served snacks: baked beans on toast or sandwiches. Sometimes Maddie put up with them, but tonight she felt hungry and decided to walk down the hill to a pizza house which stayed open until the early hours of the morning.

The street was dark and quiet. There were few people about, and the blackness between lamp-posts seemed very long. Maddie hurried from one circle of yellow light to another, wishing she had taken pot luck in the canteen. It wasn't that late, usually she passed quite a crowd coming out of a local cinema at this hour, but tonight she had missed them and a heavy shower of rain had kept most people at home.

As she turned a bend in the road she heard the footsteps behind her and glanced back. The dark shape was a young man in jeans and a leather bomber jacket. Maddie couldn't see his face, but she felt an instinctive jump of alarm; he was walking faster and she felt him watching her. She began to run; so did he. Maddie was breathing quickly, not because she was running, but because she was suddenly afraid. The sound of her own hurried breathing made her even more scared.

He was gaining on her. She felt a surge of panic, wondering if she should scream or keep running. Ahead of her lay a lighted road: shops and a steady stream of cars. If she reached that her pursuer would give up, so she put on a spurt of speed, running all out, but at the same instant he leapt to catch up with her and she felt his heavy body collide with hers.

The impact sent her flying, knocked her right off her feet. She hit her head on the pavement as she fell, and lay there only half conscious, the rain falling on her white face.

The next thing she knew was that someone had her by the shoulders and was dragging her along the wet pavement, then up a side alley which ran beside a block of shops.

Maddie struggled to get back to her feet, and the man let go of one of her shoulders, swearing.

'Shut up, Maddie!' he whispered hoarsely and hit her.

Maddie would have screamed if his leather-gloved

hand hadn't closed over her mouth a second later. She was icy cold now. He had followed her from the radio station! He knew who she was and he must have planned this—it was no chance attack, he had been waiting for her.

'Another sound from you and I'll use this,' he threatened, his other hand showing her something which flashed as he turned it.

Maddie stared incredulously at the small knife. He softly slid it along her thumb, and she saw blood spring up in a thin line. Maddie shuddered and he laughed.

'You don't want your throat cut, do you, Maddie? Just do as you're told, right? Be nice to me and I'll be nice to you.'

Sickness rose in her throat; she shut her eyes, shivering violently.

He began to pull her further into the darkness of the alley, her stockinged feet sliding on the wet ground. She must have lost her shoes in the road when she had fallen the first time.

She was trying to think; her mind chaotic. She had to get out of this, but how? She made herself go very limp; as if she had passed out. He had to tighten his hold on her to move her heavy, inert body, and as he bent a little more she threw her hands up to catch hold of his ankles and jerk him forwards hard.

He grunted and swore, but he couldn't stop himself except by letting go of her to catch the wall.

Maddie was on her feet before he could recover, and began running, screaming.

He came after her, but at that moment a car braked suddenly outside in the road. Maddie screamed louder as the man behind her leapt to get an armlock on her throat. A door slammed, and in sick relief she heard running feet heading towards her, a black figure outlined in the entrance to the alley.

Her attacker thrust her forwards and kicked her before he fled, scrambling over a wall into one of the yards behind the shops. Maddie got to her knees, swaying, white and icy, a hand to her back where she had been kicked.

'Are you OK?'

The voice was familiar; she looked up at him through a haze of tears, her lips trembling.

'It would be you, wouldn't it? Why didn't you get here five minutes ago?'

Zachary Nash knelt down beside her, his face a dark oval in the shadowy alley. She could hear the ragged drag of his breathing.

'Maddie?' He sounded strange; he sounded almost as peculiar as she felt herself. His voice had changed, deepened, become harsh. He hadn't realised it was her, and he seemed shaken.

'My God,' he muttered hoarsely, staring at her. 'What did he do to you?'

She was trembling too much to stay upright. She leaned forwards and began to cry into his tweed jacket; it was wet with rain now and smelt of sheep, a familiar, nostalgic smell from her childhood, reminding her of her father on long walks across the countryside, sudden spring showers making his old tweed jacket smell like that.

'Nothing to what he was going to do!' she hiccuped, trying to be funny when she didn't feel in the least humorous. Zachary's shoulder was warm and firm; very comforting, very solid and safe. She burrowed into him to hide and his arms came round her and held her tightly. She was safe. She cried harder, trembling from head to toe. Now that it was all over, it somehow seemed even more terrifying. While it was happening she had had fear to keep her from collapsing; now she caved in and cried it all out, clinging to Zachary.

'I got here in time,' he said above her head, yet he sounded very far away, his voice odd.

Suddenly he held her away, and reluctantly she opened her eyes, the lashes all stuck together with tears.

'What the hell were you doing walking through these streets alone at this hour, anyway?' he snarled at her, and she blinked in surprise at his sudden change of tone.

'Don't shout at me!'

'Are you stupid? Don't you know how foolhardy it is to go walking about alone at night?' He got to his feet and pulled her up with him, shaking her by the shoulders to emphasise what he was saying.

'Let go! Stop that!' Maddie yelled back, her tears drying up as she, too, began to get angry.

'You were asking for trouble!' He took her elbow and forced her back towards the street, to his parked car, and Maddie struggled to break free, seething.

'I've walked down to the pizza house hundreds of times before without running into any bother!' she threw at him.

'Then you've been lucky up to now.'

He was right, and she knew she would never risk a

walk through the dark streets again unless she had company, but she was too angry to admit it. He had no right to yell and bawl at her!

They were at his car; he opened the passenger door for her and she began to get in, then paused, frowning, looking round.

'My shoes!'

'That was what caught my attention,' remembered Zachary, looking over his shoulder. 'I saw two shoes lying in the middle of the pavement and thought it was odd, so I stopped instinctively and then I heard screaming.' He stopped, and swallowed audibly, looking down at her. 'When I think what could have happened if I hadn't been driving up to the radio station!'

He was very pale, livid; his blue eyes dark. He turned away and walked across the pavement to pick up her shoes. Maddie slid into the car, and Zachary handed her the shoes before slamming the door shut on her, as if the violence was a relief.

He got behind the wheel and turned to look at her. 'I'd like to slap you,' he said, and meant it, the words bitten out between his teeth.

Maddie had put on her shoes, and she made a face at him. 'I won't do it again,' she said, admitting it had been stupid. 'I just didn't think . . .'

'It would happen to you? Nobody ever does, and maybe you could have been lucky a thousand times or for ever—but there was always that risk and you shouldn't have taken it.'

'Because I'm a woman?' Maddie said, getting angry again.

'Yes.'

'It isn't fair!' she raged.

'I know.' Zachary watched her wryly, his mouth crooked.

'Just because I'm a woman, I'm at risk if I go out to have a meal alone after dark!'

'It may not be fair, but it's the way it is, and you mustn't take stupid risks again!' His fury had burnt itself out, and he spoke levelly.

'I interviewed someone who was running a self-defence class at the other end of town,' Maddie remembered aloud. 'I think I'll give her a ring tomorrow and join.'

'Good idea,' Zachary said, producing a large white handkerchief and wiping her tear-stained face, watching her closely. 'You're pale and there's a nasty bruise on your forehead—any other injuries?'

'No, except that I ache all over from being dragged along that hard ground.' She put a hand to her head, wincing.

'Did he hit you there?' Zachary asked harshly. Maddie shook her head, then winced again; her temples were thudding with pain.

'No, I hit it on the pavement when I fell the first time.'

'You'd better see a doctor all the same. I expect the police will insist on it.'

'The police? I can't see the point of telling them, and I don't need to see a doctor.'

'Of course you must tell the police!'

'I can't face talking about it just yet,' Maddie said huskily, biting her lip. 'Please, don't make a fuss, just drive me back.'

Zachary considered her wryly, his face uncertain, then started the engine but, instead of driving back to the radio station, he drove on down the hill and parked outside the well lit pizza house.

'I've lost my appetite,' Maddie said irritably.

'Don't let a little thing like attempted rape put you off your supper,' he said, and she glared at him, resenting the light tone until she saw the anger in his eyes. The humour was merely a cover for it. 'I like pizza myself,' he said. 'Is it good here?'

'I like it,' she said, getting out of the car, rather stiffly. She was taken aback when Zachary joined her and looked at him in alarm. 'There's no need for you to stay—I can get a taxi back, thank you.'

'There's a good table by the window,' he merely said, urging her inside, and a moment later they were ordering from the huge menu. Maddie stared through the rainy glass at the street, oddly aware of him sitting opposite her, and saw his reflection mirrored there. She hurriedly looked away.

'How do you feel now?' he asked and she shrugged.

'My head still aches,' she admitted, forcing a smile.

Zachary got up and walked away, and she stared after him in bewilderment; where was he going? She saw him talking to the waitress.

He came back with a glass of water and two white pills which he handed to her. 'Take these, that should help the head.'

She obeyed, swallowing uneasily. 'You're very kind.' Her voice was low and she watched him curiously. He was graceful for such a big man, his limbs lithe and supple under the dark suit he wore. He was no longer dressed roughly and casually; tonight he was wearing clothes which were obviously expensive. He looked quite different: clean-shaven, his hair brushed and glossy, his strong hands well manicured.

'What do you do for a living?' she asked.

'I work in the City of London,' he told her expressionlessly. 'Tell me something—how did you get into radio? How *does* one get a job like yours? There aren't that many women disc jockeys, are there?'

She smiled; it was a very frequent question from the public. 'I was lucky—my school had their own radio station, and I did a course on radio in the sixth form. When I left I was able to get a job as a trainee with a local radio station in the south of England. Of course, I never got anywhere near a mike for months—I was just a dogsbody, making tea, running around with a stopwatch, fetching and carrying. But eventually I got my chance and started broadcasting; I took over when a disc jockey was taken ill suddenly. People seemed to like me, and when he came back to work they found me another slot. I stayed there for several years, then I got a job in London with one of the commercial stations. My show was hatcheted eight months ago because it was on at the same time as a very popular show on another station. I couldn't compete, so they took me off the air—that's why I came down to Seaborough, to get another chance.'

'And you've been very successful?'

Maddie shrugged. 'I think Con's pleased with the ratings. You'd be surprised how many people listen, even though I'm on so late.'

'I'm not surprised,' he said softly, watching her. 'You have a sexy voice.'

She flushed and looked down, stupidly flustered by the compliment and amazed at herself. Men didn't get to her with a line like that; not usually, anyway. Why did she find it so hard to take from Zachary Nash?

'I'm sure you have quite a following, Maddie,' he said, and she paled again, suddenly remembering.

'He knew who I was!'

Zachary looked sharply at her, but at that moment the waitress arrived with their pizzas. She asked if they wanted anything else, but Zachary said that they didn't, for the moment, so she walked away, and Maddie met Zachary's eyes across the table.

'What do you mean, he knew who you were?'

'He called me Maddie, he must have been following me.'

'You can tell the police that,' Zachary said, his eyes hard and narrowed.

'There's no point in calling the police—I can't describe him, I never saw his face. Did you?'

'If he was following you and knew your name, he may try again,' said Zachary. 'So we'll talk to the police as soon as you've finished eating.'

'I have to get back to work as soon as I've finished eating!' Maddie said and started on her pizza, her face obstinate. She did not want to talk to the police about the attack on her; she just wanted to forget all about it, and told Zachary so, but as he drove her back to the radio station he insisted that the police must be told about the incident.

'You can talk to them tomorrow, but you must talk

to them. Next time, you might not be so lucky.' He drew up in the car park. 'How will you get home from here?'

'In my car—that's it over there.'

Zachary said flatly, 'I'll wait and see that you get home safely,' and nothing she could say would budge him on the point.

She wasn't at her best that evening; she found it hard to talk easily, to be funny or light-hearted. She kept thinking of what had happened, although, oddly enough, she wasn't thinking of the man who had attacked her but of Zachary and the reassurance she had felt as she'd cried into his wet tweed jacket. She had never been the little-woman type, clinging to a big, strong man—she was surprised at herself.

She had almost reached the end of the show when Zachary walked into the control room next door. Through the glass her eyes met his—he didn't smile, he looked very serious and that was unusual for him. She had only known him for a short time, but she knew that much about him. Zachary took life casually, he smiled a lot. So why did he look like that now?

When she joined him, he said curtly, 'I rang the police while you were on the air.'

'What did they say?' asked Maddie, frowning.

'Another girl was attacked tonight.'

'No!' she gasped, horrified.

'She was struck on the head and she's unconscious in hospital, but the police have a man in custody and they want you to identify him.'

Maddie bit her lip. 'When?'

'Tomorrow morning at ten o'clock—they'll have an identity parade and they'll want to interview you.' Zachary looked sombrely at her. 'We should have rung them right away, just after it happened—we might have made sure he didn't attack anyone else. The police would have been out there, looking for him, and they might have picked him up before he got to this other girl.'

Maddie flinched. 'Was she raped?' she whispered, sick with guilt at the realisation that she might be to blame for this other attack.

'No, she was lucky, like you,' he admitted flatly. 'Someone heard screaming and rang the police, and a police car happened to be nearby—but the principle's the same, Maddie. It could have been very different.'

She put her hands over her face as tears welled up in her eyes; she couldn't stop them but she wouldn't cry in front of him.

There was a silence while she fought to stop the tears, then Zachary moved. She felt his arm go round her, his cheek against her hair.

'Don't,' he said in a low voice, his mouth muffled by her hair. 'Don't cry, Maddie.' The anger she had felt in him had burnt out; his voice was gentle, reassuring, and Maddie let herself lean on him. It was comforting, but she mustn't make a habit of turning to this man for comfort; she might start to depend on it and that would be fatal. He would vanish soon, as suddenly as he had appeared in her life. She must not start liking him too much.

CHAPTER FOUR

MADDIE woke up the following morning with a sense of doom for which she could not account for a second or two. At first she told herself that it must be Friday, the day on which Con held the weekly meeting to which all programme staff were summoned. Con called it the budget briefing—the staff called it a great many other things, none of them complimentary. Money was of paramount importance to the radio station; its income from advertising fluctuated by the season since this was a seaside resort and the population in winter was mostly low while in summer it was often twice the size. In winter, therefore, Con kept a strict eye on costs, and complained bitterly if they rose, which meant that the programme staff had to cut their programmes to the bone. Even Maddie was affected, since Con warned her to talk more in winter and play slightly fewer records—the resulting saving in needle time wasn't much, but every little helped, he said, ignoring what Maddie had said in reply.

Opening one wary eye, Maddie peered at the calendar on her wall; it *was* Friday and there would be a meeting at eleven, but that was not what was oppressing her. It was eight o'clock; she had only had about four hours' sleep, she had a headache and at ten o'clock she had to be at the police station for this identity parade.

She was not looking forward to it. In fact, she was dreading it; seeing that man again would remind her of a few minutes she would much rather forget. She had been lucky, it could have been far worse, but Maddie would rather have forgotten about it. What had happened had been quite bad enough; she had been afraid of having nightmares and was unsurprised when she did.

It had been hard to get to sleep at all. She had lain awake, listening, nerves stretched, startled by every tiny sound. The familiar had become the terrible: the wail of a cat somewhere, the creak of a floorboard in another flat, the sound of the sea, the gurgle of running water—all ordinary little sounds in themselves, yet tonight invested with terror.

Maddie had always prized herself on her common sense and toughness. She had had the guts to leave home, to live alone, to move away from her family and everything she knew—she wouldn't have believed that she could get so edgy.

Now she was yawning and dying to get back to sleep, but she had to get up because at nine-forty Zachary Nash would be here to drive her to the police station. He had driven her home last night, insisting that she left her own car in the office car park. Maddie had put up a token protest, but secretly had been rather relieved to have his escort home. He had even come up here with her and stood in the door of the flat while she put on every light and checked every room.

He was an intelligent, thoughtful man; she couldn't deny it, and wondered why she found him at the same time so maddening. His very intelligence made him a worrying adversary; his mockery and the teasing of his quick glance put her back up and Zachary knew it. He deliberately provoked her—why?

Sliding one foot out of bed, she reluctantly started to get up. It was chilly this morning, and when she looked out of the window she discovered that it was grey and rainy, too. The sea had a sullen look; it suited her mood and she glared back at it.

Her flat was in a modern block on the sea front; it had been purpose-built, with holiday letting in mind, but the owner had had trouble with the succession of holiday-makers who took the place in season, and so he had put the flat up for rent to a full-time tenant. Maddie had been delighted to get it; it wasn't too expensive, it was close to her job, and it was modern and comfortably furnished. She had made a few changes, of course: some pictures, ornaments, plant-pots everywhere to give a garden effect in the living room and bathroom, and a little row of potted herbs on the kitchen window. She had made the place her own by now.

It was the view that made it spectacular, though—Maddie was on the second floor and her windows looked over the changing sea, giving her full time entertainment night and day.

When she had dressed and eaten a tiny breakfast, she rang Enid, Con's secretary, to explain why she might be late for the weekly meeting.

'The police station? Why?' Enid was instantly agog, her voice squeaking a little.

'A guy attacked me last night, in the street—no, I wasn't hurt,' she said in response to Enid's gasp of horror. 'Luckily, someone else came along, and the guy ran off, but the police picked him up and I've got to try to identify him.'

'What happened?' asked Enid, and Maddie pulled a face. She had known she would be deluged with questions when she told Enid, but expecting it didn't make it any easier to deal with.

'Nothing much, thank heavens. Sorry, I must rush, Enid. Tell Con I'll get there as soon as I can.'

She hung up while Enid was boiling with curiosity, and sighed with relief. She was going to have to put up with cross-examination by the police; she didn't feel she could go through that twice.

Enid would have the story all round the building by the time she finally got to work, of course—much exaggerated and embroidered. She hadn't given Enid much material to work with, but Enid wouldn't worry about that! What she didn't know she would invent, just as she had made up so much of the gossip about Con and his wife. Most people in the firm had got their idea of Jill from Enid. How much trouble had Enid caused between them? Maddie wondered wryly. It was so easy to pass on a wrong message—garble words, change phrasing, give a false impression—and Enid had a strong motive for wanting to wreck Con's marriage. Everyone knew how Enid felt about Con; she didn't hide it. No doubt Con was so used to her that it no longer really impinged on his awareness. She was like the office wallpaper to him, but she wasn't just that, was she? She was a jealous, vindictive woman, and Con had made a deadly mistake in discounting her.

The doorbell rang and Maddie jumped about six feet in the air. My nerves are in a state! she thought resentfully, feeling them jangling in a chain reaction. It must be the after-effects of last night, she wasn't back to normal yet.

She was expecting to see Zachary Nash outside the door, so she couldn't think why the sight of him should make her feel hollow inside, as though she might float away if she didn't hang on to something. It had to be the shock; how much longer did these strange effects last?

'Good morning,' he said in that deep voice, staring at her as if she had three heads.

'You're late,' she accused.

'Every time I see you, you're scowling,' he said. 'You're a very aggressive female.'

'I'm nothing of the kind!' she flared, reddening.

His gaze wandered down to her clenched fists. 'No?'

She considered hitting him with them for a second, then forced them open and let them hang at her side. 'No,' she said, banging her front door shut and walking past him. If she was aggressive whenever they met it was because he provoked her into it, but she was going to stay cool today. She had an ordeal in front of her, and Zachary Nash wasn't going to make it worse with his wicked blue eyes and teasing smile.

'You look very businesslike,' he said as they drove away from the sea and into town. 'A shrewd choice for meeting the police.'

Maddie didn't answer, but buttoned her topcoat to hide the dove-grey jersey dress with its high neckline and straight skirt. She hadn't had the police in mind; she had been dressing as camouflage, removing herself as far as she could from what had happened last night. She hadn't even been aware of it until Zachary Nash drew her attention to it, but she resented his awareness and shrewdness. She wished he would stop exploring her private thoughts, guessing at her motives. It was disturbing.

He was formally dressed, too, though—from strategy? Had he picked out the charcoal pin-striped suit, and severe dark red tie against a city shirt of red stripes on white—to make a point with the police, visibly demonstrate his honesty and position in the world?

Maddie eyed him sideways under her lashes, her mouth crooked with humour. Human beings could be very predictable and very odd, especially the male of the species.

'What?' he asked, and her lashes lifted a little.

'What?'

'Are you thinking?'

'Why?'

'You were looking at me in a way I'm not sure I like.'

'Sorry,' she said sweetly, giving him an insincere smile.

He laughed. 'You're not, you liar.'

'No, I'm not,' she admitted, her smoky-grey eyes wide and glittering.

'Don't, if you're wise,' Zachary said very softly.

'Don't what?'

'Look at me like that,' he said in a husky voice, and she was instantly breathless.

'I wasn't aware of looking at you in any particular way,' she said, however, fighting to keep her voice level.'

'Oh, yes, you were,' said Zachary, his mouth indenting. 'You looked at me in a very particular way and you know it. If you keep issuing challenges, Maddie, don't be surprised if they get taken up.' He turned a corner and almost ran into a car coming the other way on their side of the road. Zachary swore, his attention forced back to the road, and Maddie struggled to breathe normally again. This was getting serious, and she didn't like it. She barely knew the man. If she had been in her teens and ripe to fall in love at first sight for the first time, she could have understood it—but she was twenty-five, of sound mind and possessing a great deal of common sense. She had had boyfriends and never lost her head over one of them. She wasn't the type to go crazy over a man, particularly not a stranger.

What on earth was happening to her?

Zachary drew up outside the police station in the wide, leafy avenue close to the centre of town, then turned to look at her, one arm sliding along the back of the seat.

'How do you feel?'

Maddie swallowed, her eyes dropping in front of

that blue stare. That was the very last thing she would ever tell *him!* Or did he already know? At times, she was sure he did know how he made her feel—at others, she wasn't certain. He had her confused—bewildered and bewitched.

'Ready to face the police?' added Zachary, and she caught back her betraying sigh of relief.

'Oh. Yes.' She grimaced. 'Well, as ready as I'll ever be.' She wasn't looking forward to it, of course. Her stomach churned at the very thought of telling her story, answering the questions that would inevitably follow—and then having to go through the identity parade.

'Nervous?' Zachary asked gently, and she shrugged, eyes down.

He put a finger under her chin and lifted her face so that she couldn't help looking at him.

'It will be over before you know it,' he said, a smile in his blue eyes. 'Think of it as a visit to the dentist—nasty but necessary.'

'I'm not a child, you know,' she said wryly.

'Oh, I *know,*' he said in a soft voice, his eyes running down over her. Maddie caught her breath, immediately aware of her body and of how he was looking at it.

Before she could react, though, he moved again, suddenly leaning over her and kissing her, his mouth warm and firm against her parted, startled lips. It wasn't a passionate or a demanding kiss. It was a reassurance, a caress, over before she knew it had begun.

She found him gone a second later. He got out of

the car and came round to open her door. Maddie stumbled out on to the pavement, pink and shaky, still feeling the touch of his mouth on her own even as she avoided meeting his eyes while they walked into the police station. She wasn't scared any more—Zachary had given her quite another problem to brood over. In fact, she found it hard to concentrate on her statement because she kept thinking about that quick, warm touch of his mouth, and each time it made her heart give a funny little sideways kick, like a horse about to bolt.

The identity parade was difficult. The men all looked alike at first but, as Maddie paused in front of one man, she picked up a scent from him that was familiar. She looked at him, but his eyes were fixed over her shoulder, he wouldn't meet her stare. Maddie almost shut her eyes and let her instincts work. She couldn't exactly place his face, but it had been dark and she had been too scared to notice much.

She told the police she thought that might be the man but she wasn't a hundred per cent sure.

'It was dark and I didn't see much of his face, but I definitely got a niggling feeling that that was him. The height and build were right, and he was wearing a cheap aftershave or something—that much I am sure about, that man smelt like that.'

The sergeant was resigned and not too unhappy. They had the other girl as a witness, so they thanked Maddie and she left with Zachary to drive back to the radio station and pick up her car.

'It's lunch time—why don't we have lunch first?'

Zachary asked as they drove, and Maddie almost accepted until it dawned on her that she had another date.

'Oh, no, it's Friday,' she groaned, and Zachary's brows lifted.

'Does that have some special significance?'

'I'm having lunch with someone else today. I'd forgotten all about it,' she said. 'It's lucky you reminded me.'

'Is it?' he drawled, and Maddie gave him a second look, picking up on the dry intonation—he didn't believe her, he thought she was just inventing her date as an excuse.

'Thanks for asking, anyway,' she said politely. Actually, she was relieved now that she had escaped the dangers of spending any more time alone with him. She had been about to accept, and that would have been a mistake. Zachary Nash was as insidious as ivy—he grew on you and she had a sinking suspicion that he might strangle the life out of you in the process! She had only known him such a short time, yet she felt she had known him for years, and that was crazy. It was a delusion, one she felt he had put into her head. She knew nothing whatever about him; more than that, whenever she asked him about himself his answers seemed as illuminating as a blank wall. He was secretive and evasive, and she did not trust him, but she gave him a cool smile.

'How about dinner tonight, then?' he asked, and she hesitated.

'Well . . .' Over a meal she would get the chance to ask him a few more questions and find out more, but she was oddly afraid of seeing him again.

'I'll pick you up at your flat at seven,' he steam-rollered on as if she had accepted, turning into the car park of the radio station.

Maddie could have invented some other engagement, but while she was thinking about it, torn this way and then another, Zachary had pulled up next to her car and had got out, and the moment was gone.

He came round and opened the passenger door for her. 'Got your car key?'

She found it and got out, still hesitating, but before she could come to a decision Zachary walked back to the other side of his car and got behind the wheel.

'See you tonight,' he said, and Maddie opened and shut her mouth like a stupid goldfish while he drove off. Apparently, he was quite oblivious of her uncertainty, or was he? Maddie frowned after him, wondering about that. Had he left so suddenly to make sure that she didn't get around to inventing another excuse for turning down a date with him?

While she was still debating that, Con appeared and strode across the car park to where she stood lost in thought. Con was scowling and black-browed, and his voice made her jump.

'What the hell's all this about you being mugged last night?'

'Oh!' she said, shaken by his aggression. 'Oh, hello, Con.' And then she flushed and told him what had happened.

Con exploded at her as if she had invited the whole thing. 'What on earth made you walk the streets alone at that hour?' he accused, and she bristled.

'I didn't go out looking for trouble, if that's what you're implying. This isn't London, after all—or any city, come to that. It's a peaceful little seaside town out of season—how was I to guess that some nut was lurking about out there? It wasn't even that late, not even eleven o'clock at night.'

'Well, in future . . .' Con began, glowering at her in that way he had, and she glared back resentfully.

'Don't lecture me, Con. I don't need any dark warnings, I'm not stupid. This is a sick world we're living in, and much as I resent being under virtual house arrest, I'll try to avoid risks from now on, but just don't hassle me!'

Con considered her, his face changing. 'I'm sorry, Maddie. I've been worried sick ever since Enid told me—I rang the police and talked to them and got their side of the story. Thank heavens you weren't badly hurt, anyway. I got the impression from Enid that . . .' He stopped, grimacing.

Maddie could fill in the gap—trust Enid to imagine the worst and embroider the story for Con.

'I've got a headache, a piece of sticking plaster on my head and a few bruises and bumps, that's all,' she said. 'I'm fine—so can we just forget about it, now? Is the meeting over?'

He nodded, still watching her with a frown.

'Anything vital I should know about?' she insisted, ignoring that stare.

'Enid will be sending you the minutes of the meeting.'

'Oh, good,' she said sarcastically.

Con laughed. 'I'm glad you're OK, Maddie,' he said abruptly. 'How about some lunch? I was just on my way to eat.'

She exclaimed, looking at her watch. 'Sorry, Con—I've got a date with Jack, and I'm going to be late if I don't hurry. See you.'

Jack had heard the news, too, she found—Enid had been busy. He looked anxious and embarrassed. 'I didn't think you'd turn up,' he said. 'I tried to ring, but you were out all morning.'

Maddie set him straight about the over-colourful version Enid had given him, but she was tired of talking about it all by then and the lunch was a disaster. They talked in a desultory fashion about work, politics, films and the cost of living, but she kept wishing she was somewhere else. She liked Jack well enough, but she could take him or leave him, and she sensed Jack wasn't too happy, either.

'We must do this again soon,' he said unconvincingly as they left, but he didn't try to pin her down to a date or time. Jack had been upset by the story of the mugging; Maddie was a news story happening in his own back yard and Jack was uneasy about the whole thing. He didn't want to be involved; she had become red-hot for him and he was dropping her.

She was glad that didn't bother her, although it would have been all the same if it had, she guessed. Jack was that sort of man, he hated being embarrassed and uneasy. He liked his life simple and uncomplicated. He was a good engineer; he wanted his life to work as smoothly as his machines, and as predictably. He wasn't a rat, more a rabbit—and he was ducking back down his burrow at speed!

Maddie spent ages deciding what to wear that evening because, though she wasn't sure why, her mind seemed to be in a state of utter confusion. She put on one dress, changed her mind and put on another, then flicked through her wardrobe impatiently, looking for something else—but nothing she owned pleased her. She had nothing to wear, not a rag to her back.

It's only a guy I barely know, she told her reflection in the mirror. What does it matter?

She hadn't bothered for Jack; she had worn the demure dove-grey for the police station without even considering whether Jack would approve of it. Of course, she wasn't dressing for Zachary Nash, nor did his opinion matter a damn to her, but tonight she wanted to look special, and her flushed face and glittering eyes were worrying. What was the matter with her?

She pulled a dress out of the wardrobe: peacock-blue and shimmering with sequins. It was flashy, she thought, teeth tight, but it made her look very alive. She wouldn't go unnoticed tonight, with her black hair sleek and her figure smoothly emphasised by the clinging silk of the dress.

She met the aware brilliance of her own eyes with irony. What are you hoping to do? she asked herself. Make him stare? Aren't you past the stage of trying to dazzle men? Adolescents hope for that, you're a big girl now, so grow up!

The trouble was, she felt like an adolescent tonight:

her skin hot and her heartbeats crazy as she looked down from her flat window and saw Zachary's car pull up.

She had never felt like this before, never, not even as a teenager. What did she know about the man? Why did he make her feel like this?

OK, he's attractive, she thought, as he walked across the pavement, unaware of her watching him. But so what? You've known plenty of other men just as good-looking, and it hasn't done this to you.

Was it some sort of passing illness? A fever brought on by too many broken nights, too little sleep, the odd events of the past few days—was that what this was?

The doorbell went and her body shook violently—fever, she told herself hastily, in agitation—that's all this is, a passing fever, it means nothing. It will go as fast as it came.

She opened the door and Zachary smiled at her, and Maddie's temperature shot sky-high.

'You look fantastic,' he said in that deep, warm voice.

So did he—elegant in a well cut dark suit and white shirt. He looked cool and sexy, and Maddie felt her head swim. This was frightening, she didn't know if she could cope with the way she felt.

'Thank you,' she managed to say huskily, not adding that he looked terrific, too. No doubt he knew it; he was one of those men, self-assured, saturated with confidence and used to getting his own way.

He held the car door open while she got into the passenger seat. She knew he was watching her legs, but pretended to be blind. The weather had improved during the afternoon, the sky was cloudless and it was warmer. Maddie leaned back in the passenger seat while Zachary drove. She stared up at the stars—she had never seen them look so bright or so close. You could almost touch them.

'You're quiet,' he said softly. 'Tired?'

'No,' she said, not answering the real question. She was feeling so very odd and she was extraordinarily happy, it was terrifying how happy she was, and all for nothing. She felt she was floating, utterly weightless.

He took her to the restaurant at which she had dined with Con only the other night. The head waiter recognised her, but discreetly said nothing, although his smile was curious and intrigued—two different men in one week?

Zachary noticed that look, of course. He would. He saw everything.

'I gather you're well known here,' was all he said as they began to study the menu.

'This isn't my first visit,' she admitted, shrugging.

He smiled wryly. 'You get around, don't you? Are there many men in your life?'

She shrugged again and consulted the menu. 'The soup sounds good, unusual, too. I think I'll start with that—it's not too high in calories.'

He let her change the subject; they ordered, and while they waited Maddie talked about Jill Osborne.

'What is she doing? A career, I gather?'

'Yes,' he said, watching her in a way that made her doubly nervous. 'Did your lunch date bring you here?'

She was saved the problem of answering by the arrival of their first course, but if she thought he would forget the question she soon found she had under estimated him.

'Is he special?' he asked a moment later, and she felt her hand shake, lifting soup to her mouth. Some spilled and she made a great business of mopping the table-cloth.

'Why assume I had lunch with a man?' she asked, quarrelsome on the surface, scowling, although underneath she was see-sawing between that powerful attraction towards him and a strange hostility. It was an absurd muddle to be in, and Maddie resented her own emotions, resented him, too. Zachary was the sole cause of the way she felt, after all, and she sensed he was aware of it.

'Did you?' he merely insisted, and it was stupid to deny it, almost as stupid as it had been to evade his question in the first place.

'Yes,' she admitted grudgingly, and he laughed.

'Not hard to guess—so is he? Special?'

'No,' she said, and Zachary put down his knife and fork and looked at her across their table. She was suddenly breathless, her heart racing. He smiled, and her heart started banging about inside her chest until it hurt.

'Is anyone?' he asked, his voice deep, and she couldn't stop herself from shaking her head.

He smiled again and her mouth went dry. 'Good,' he said very softly.

She pulled herself together, stiffening her back. 'Why the interest?'

'As if you didn't know!' he mocked, and Maddie bit her lip.

'What about you? You keep asking me leading

questions, but you never tell me anything about yourself.'

'Ask away,' he said. 'There's nothing to tell—I've been waiting for that special person, the one who's what I'm looking for . . .'

'How special does she have to be?' Maddie asked drily, and he laughed.

'I don't have a shopping list, that wasn't what I meant. I always knew I'd recognise her when I saw her, that's all, and I never did.'

Until now? she wondered, meeting his eyes across the table. She felt helpless and defenceless at that instant, because she wasn't hiding anything from him and he was looking directly into her smoky-grey eyes and down inside her very soul. Was that what he was saying? That she was what he had been looking for?

She felt herself trembling, and his hand moved across the table, found hers, held it, lifted it.

Maddie watched, wide-eyed and dry-mouthed as he gently kissed her hand, his lips moving on the warm palm.

It was then that someone walking past stopped abruptly beside their table. Maddie vaguely heard a muffled exclamation, wordless, a rough intake of air. Zachary looked round and a second later let go of her hand. Dazedly, Maddie looked round too.

'Con!' She almost didn't recognise him. His face was so strange: white and tight-lipped.

He wasn't even looking at her, though. She got the feeling he hadn't even realised she was there. He was staring fixedly at Zachary as if he wanted to kill him; his eyes were glittering, savage.

'You!' he muttered. 'So you *are* here with her!'

Zachary didn't answer. He was frowning, and looked oddly unsure of himself. Maddie couldn't understand this. She looked from one to the other of them, puzzled. What was going on?

That was when she moved slightly, and Con heard her and looked her way briefly, turned back to Zachary and instantly, in a double-take, looked at Maddie again.

'Maddie?' His voice was a whisper, incredulous. 'What are *you* doing here? With *him?* I didn't think you'd ever met him. You've never mentioned meeting him.'

Maddie just stared, wondering what he was talking about, and Con stared back at her, his face working violently.

'When did you meet him?' he asked, thinking aloud rather than asking her the question. 'I suppose it was him at the house when you went there? Why didn't you tell me? You didn't say who Jill had sent.'

It was Maddie's turn to look stricken, to start and turn disbelieving, angry eyes on Zachary. She didn't need to ask aloud the question in her mind—she read the answer in his pale face.

Con saw her expression and asked curtly, 'You didn't know?' Con knew her well by now, and he read that look in her face. 'He didn't tell you who he was?'

'Zachary Nash, he said his name was Zachary Nash,' she whispered.

Con smiled, his mouth cold and thin-lipped. 'Oh, that's his name. He's my half-brother, and he took my wife away from me.'

CHAPTER FIVE

CON drove her to the radio station. Maddie hadn't said a word to Zachary Nash after Con had dropped his bombshell—one look at Zachary had told her it was true and she had walked out of the restaurant, leaving him at the table. She had never felt such pain; it was like an amputation, she thought, leaning on the wall outside in the darkness, fighting to recover control of herself. This must be how you felt when you lost part of yourself. Maddie had never felt pain like it before, and she didn't know how to handle it.

Con had joined her and frowned down at her, a tentative hand on her arm. 'Are you OK?'

'Can you give me a lift to work, please, Con?' she had managed, surprised to hear her voice sounding so normal. Did her face look that ordinary? She felt as if all the blood had drained from her heart, let alone her face, but Con didn't seem horror-stricken by what he saw. He simply nodded.

'My car's across the road.'

She wondered briefly if she could walk; her knees were giving and she felt weak, but she made it to Con's car without too much of an effort, not visibly, anyway. Con had his arm round her, though, so he must have noticed more than he appeared to do, and she felt his concern tangibly as he slid her into the passenger seat as tenderly as if she were an invalid.

It wasn't until they were in the car park outside the radio station that Con asked quietly, 'Why were you having dinner with him?'

'I've seen him several times since I met him at your house,' Maddie said. 'But as I didn't realise he was your brother, it didn't occur to me that . . .' She broke off, biting her lip. 'Oh, I'm so angry! How could he lie . . . and your wife! Why didn't she say something?'

'Jill?' Con looked sharply at her. 'You've met her? But I thought she didn't come to the house? That's what you told me.'

'She didn't, but Zach . . . he took me back to his hotel and she was there.' Maddie shut her eyes, breathing with effort. 'She was there—I'm so stupid! It didn't enter my head that they . . .'

'They're staying at the hotel together?' Con asked in a flat, drained voice.

Maddie nodded; she couldn't speak. She hadn't picked up any vibes from Zachary and Jill Osborne. They acted like friends, not lovers. What sort of people were they? Jill must have realised that Zachary was showing signs of interest in Maddie. After all, he had brought her back to the hotel and he had flirted, hadn't he? She sat in the car in silence, remembering that meeting, the teasing mockery in his eyes and the sexual tension between them. She remembered Jill Osborne's look of surprise, too, the way her brows had gone up and she had stared. Had she been jealous? She hadn't shown it. Far from it;

she had seemed amused, she had laughed and watched them indulgently. How could she, if she was having an affair with Zachary herself?

Maddie couldn't help being puzzled. She had been so convinced by the sadness in Jill's eyes when she'd talked about Con. She had been left with the fixed impression that Jill was still in love with him and not involved with any other man; that the break-up of their marriage was just a tragic mistake, a confusion somehow, something that could be put right if someone could only get them together again.

'Are you sure?' she asked Con huskily.

'About what?'

'That they . . . went away together?'

'Of course I'm sure—I didn't see them go, but plenty of others did and, anyway, they have always been close. He knew her before I did. For all I know, he was in love with her years ago and just didn't get around to making it clear.' Con's mouth twisted and he scowled blackly. 'Maybe they even had an affair —how do I know? I thought she loved me. I could have been wrong. Who knows why she married me? All I know is that he came here and she left with him—and they're here now together, so they have obviously been together since Jill left me.'

Watching his familiar glower, it occurred to Maddie for the first time that there really was some fugitive resemblance between him and Zachary, not so much in colouring or build, but now and then in expression, in the way their eyes blazed or their brows drew together. You had to catch that resemblance in motion, one flash of likeness and it was gone again, but it was definitely there. She would eventually have guessed that they were related.

'You said he was your half-brother?' she queried, and Con nodded.

'By my mother's first marriage.'

'Her first husband died?'

'A pity he didn't!' Con's voice was harsh. 'No, he was just a selfish swine who had affairs right from the start of their marriage. My mother put up with it for a few years because of their child. They only had one, Zachary. When my mother couldn't bear it any longer she left, taking him with her, but of course she couldn't win against the Nash money. Her husband was a very rich man, and he used his money ruthlessly. In court she found herself being accused of every crime under the sun: affairs, drinking, even drugs—they threw everything they could think of at her and some of the mud stuck. She was crucified by his lawyers.'

Maddie watched Con with compassion. His face was livid and his eyes bitterly angry.

'I wish you had met my mother,' he said. 'She was a lovely lady—gentle and vulnerable. They put her through a wringer and she lost custody of her son. It broke her up. Even though she met my father a couple of years later and remarried, she was never really happy. You could see it in her eyes, even when she was smiling. The Nash family ruined her life with their damn money. My father wasn't a poor man, he had a sound business and we lived comfortably—but we weren't in the same class.'

Con paused, his face grim. *'Then!'* he added. 'One day we will be, if I have anything to do with it. Zachary Nash took my wife away from me the way his father took him away from my mother—but I intend to be as big and as powerful as either him or his father. And then we'll see.'

Maddie felt a leap of comprehension. So that explained Con's drive and ambition? He wanted to compete with his half-brother and his mother's first husband? She looked uneasily at him; it was a dangerous reason for chasing success.

'Is Mr Nash alive? Zachary's father?' she asked, and Con shook his head, almost regretfully.

'No, he died just before my mother did. I sometimes wish he was still around, to see my family business get bigger and bigger. He sneered at my father the only time they met, patronised him. He wouldn't be able to do that now. The firm is growing by leaps and bounds.'

'Did you and Zachary meet when you were children?'

Con grimaced. 'Rarely. She was supposed to have access—as the social workers call it now—but of course his father did everything he could to make it hard for her to see him. He was put in boarding school at the other end of the country. She could only see him for a few hours, but it took her a whole weekend because she had to stay the night, she couldn't get there and back in a day. Oh, Nash didn't mean her to see their son very often, and he didn't want Zachary to meet *me* at all. It was only years later, when Zachary was at university, that we *did* meet, and then we hated each other on sight.'

'How old were you?'

'Nearly eleven. Old enough to understand why my mother cried when she saw him.' Con's voice was tight, his face pale.

Had he been jealous of his half-brother? He must have been curious, that was only human—but had he felt threatened, too, by this brother he had never met but who had been his mother's first son, and for whom she must have longed? Had his mother often talked about Zachary? Had she shown some preference, without realising it? Children were instinctively possessive, instinctively jealous, mused Maddie, even of someone they had never met but who seemed to be in competition with them. Or had Con's father shown resentment, jealousy, dislike of his wife's first husband, first son? Children picked up adult emotions even when they weren't spoken or shown. They were like little radar sets; quivering antennae picking up every tiny nuance.

'So Zachary is quite a bit older than you?' Maddie murmured, and Con nodded.

'Seven years between us—nearly eight, actually.'

So Zachary was thirty-seven or thirty-eight? He didn't look that old, and Maddie was surprised, for he had no strands of silver in his hair, no telltale lines around the mouth or eyes.

'How come he knew Jill before you did?' she asked, and Con shrugged.

'He knew her family—in fact, he introduced us. I met Jill in London at a trade fair cocktail party. Zachary was there with her. His company is a huge electronics firm, and Jill was working for them in public relations. I rang her up and asked her out and . . .' He paused, pulling a face. 'And we got married just a few months later.'

'That was quick!' Maddie said, smiling, but Con didn't smile back. His face was sombre as he nodded.

'Too quick. We didn't look before we leapt.'

Maddie felt instinctive sympathy for him, the pain was showing in his eyes again, but her mind was working on more than one level now that she had met Jill and Zachary Nash and she could see the situation in sharper focus. It was all more complex and more blurred than she had at first supposed, but then things generally were. She sighed, and Con looked sharply at her.

'What?'

'Nothing,' she said, not wanting to tell him what she had just thought. Con's childhood and family background had made him very unhappy, and you could understand that—but what had it done to Zachary? He had been the child caught between quarrelling parents: a weapon they had used, a battleground they fought over, torn first this way and then that.

What had that done to him? How did he feel about Con, the child of his mother's second marriage? Was he as jealous of Con as Con was of him? Had Con, in fact, stolen Jill from Zachary? Con said that his half-brother had introduced them at a party, that Zachary had known her long before that and might well have been in love with her. Con glossed over how his marriage began, he wasn't admitting that he had deliberately set out to steal Zachary's girlfriend—but wasn't that what he had done?

She looked at her watch, frowning. 'I must go and get my show organised,' she said, and Con looked surprised.

'Is it that late?'

'Yes.' They had been talking for a long time; their silences as eloquent as their actual words. However, although Maddie knew far more about him and his family now, she knew that for every answer she had got she had discovered another ten questions she would like answered. She turned to get out of the car, and Con put a hand on her arm.

'Don't ring for a taxi to take you home after the show—I'll make sure a car is waiting for you.'

'Thank you.'

'And don't go out for supper, eat in the canteen. I've talked to the canteen manager, and from now on there will be more than beans on toast available. Salad or something easy, anyway.'

Maddie grinned at him. 'OK, thanks.' She opened the car door and slid out, and Con leaned over to say something more.

'I'll be listening. I'm one of your biggest fans. The show's great.'

She went a little pink and laughed. 'Well, thank you.' He had never said that before, and Maddie was touched and delighted.

He drove away before she was inside the building, and she glanced back over her shoulder at his vanishing tail-lights. Once they had gone, the little town seemed more silent than ever, asleep and shuttered in the dark, with the sound of the sea rising above the faint noise of the traffic. There were few cars about at this hour, few people, too. At night the sea came into its own, breathing gently in the darkness or, on stormy nights, thundering up on to the beaches and crashing on to the jagged rocks. Wherever you were in town you could never forget the sea; it was a permanent presence on the ear and the salt-laden air you breathed, and from almost all parts of the town you saw it, too, changing colours in the changing light—now blue, now grey, now green, and sometimes almost black.

Maddie went up in the lift into her studio and set about getting her show together, but she was always aware of the town and the sea, out there in the night, waiting for her voice to start murmuring on the airwaves. It was all so peaceful on the surface, but she knew danger lurked underneath, as it had the night she'd been attacked in those quiet streets, or if you ran on to those jagged rocks which the sea covered at high tide.

She worked instinctively, on automatic pilot, her mind free to wander back to what was really obsessing her at the moment, the tangled situation between Con and his wife and Zachary Nash.

She would love to know the truth about how Zachary felt, both about his half-brother and about Jill Osborne. Had he been in love with her before she had met Con? Had it been a blow to him when she'd suddenly married his half-brother? Had he come down here deliberately to steal her back? Had they been living together in London and, if so, why on earth had he gone out of his way to flirt with *her?* And why had Jill watched complacently, without seeming to mind?

It was puzzling, and Maddie ached to know all the answers to those interminable questions, but meanwhile she read through the latest batch of listener mail, picked out those she wanted to answer on the air, put them in order to read out between discs, flipped through the day's newspapers to choose the news stories to mention on the show and wrote out her usual scribbled notes. Several people came wandering in to chat, mainly staff gossip about friends and acquaintances. It was an average night and a pretty average show; she coasted through it without feeling very excited and that was disturbing, in a way, because her flat mood was unusual for her. She relied on her easy flow of chat to get her through each night, and tonight she had to force it. A lot of her cheerfulness was pretence, and she wasn't 'high' when she came off the air—in fact, she walked out of the studio feeling distinctly low.

She would have liked to believe that it was just the after-effects of all the shocks she had had that week. A lot had happened to her in a very short time; of course she felt odd—what could you expect? She told herself she had merely used up all her energy and was feeling drained, but that after a weekend off she would feel fine again. A couple of good nights' sleep, hours of doing nothing much . . . wasn't that all she needed?

She realised it wasn't that simple. Her depression

had another root and she knew it. The biggest shock that had hit her that week was human and had a name—Zachary Nash, he was her real problem. Against her better judgement, in the face of all common sense, she had been fool enough to start falling in love. It was her first time; she had never felt like that before, a wild, piercing sweetness that was both pleasure and pain, an excitement that made her feel feverish, an awareness that made her ultra-sensitive to him and to everything around her. She couldn't describe it any other way; suddenly she had felt she saw colours more brightly, objects more clearly, felt things more deeply. She was up there walking on the sky—and then suddenly she had tumbled and she was down in the depths, drowning in misery.

She had vertigo merely remembering how fast it had all happened. Only a few days ago she hadn't even heard of Zachary Nash. Happy days! she thought, her teeth together. Hard to believe now, that her life had once been so blissful. And empty.

What was she thinking about? Of course it hadn't been empty! Simply uneventful. Not any more, though; in a very short time she had been through whole galaxies of emotions, from irritation to passion. Now she just hated him.

Wait till I see him again! she thought, blackly scowling, as she went home in the chauffeur-driven car she had found waiting for her. Con had remembered to arrange it; he was a good man to work for! He was a good man altogether. He didn't deserve what his wife and his-half brother had done to him.

Zachary Nash was a swine, a ruthless, amoral,

lying, cheating swine—and she would tell him so next time she saw him.

She got into bed, still compiling lists of his flaws—it took hours. She didn't get to sleep until dawn, and even then she was restless. Her bedclothes were all over the place when she woke up; she was hot and ached from head to foot, she had a headache and bells were ringing.

For a moment she was too disorientated to realise that one of the bells, at least, was real, then she stumbled out of the bed and shouldered into a dressing-gown. Yawning and dishevelled, she got to the front door.

She had actually started to pull it open before it occurred to her that it might be Zachary on the doorstep. Her body froze and she turned icy, half inclined to slam the door shut again—then she moved to look through the gap and it wasn't him standing there. It was Jill Osborne.

'Oh!' she said, startled.

'Hello,' Jill said quietly. 'Can I come in? I have to talk to you.'

Maddie stepped back, opening the door wide, and Jill walked past her. Maddie gestured to the tiny sitting-room.

'Please . . .'

She shut the front door and hovered in the corridor, watching Jill walk across the room.

'I'm sorry, I've only just got up—can I make you some coffee? I'm dying for some.'

'Please,' Jill said huskily, turning to look back at her. She was pale and looked as tired as Maddie felt.

'I'm sorry if I woke you—I didn't realise that . . .' Her voice trailed off hopelessly, and Maddie smiled wryly at her.

'Don't worry, I'm normally up by this time—this morning was an exception. Sit down. I won't be a moment.'

Jill sat down and Maddie rushed into the kitchen, put on coffee and set out cups, tore back down the corridor to wash her face, clean her teeth and brush her hair, and about five minutes later was back in the kitchen, wearing blue denim jeans and a thin white sweater. She felt a little more human, anyway.

She carried a tray through into the sitting-room and found Jill on her feet again, exploring her bookcases. Jill turned with an apologetic smile.

'Sorry, I can never resist books.'

'Neither can I. My collection is pretty eclectic.'

'I'm never sure what that means,' said Jill, sitting down again and accepting a cup of black coffee.

Maddie flushed, reading irony into the remark. 'Oh, I read odd books, very personal tastes—do you take milk?'

Jill did. 'No sugar, though.'

Maddie offered her a plate of Digestive biscuits. Jill took one, and there was a brief silence while Maddie settled herself down.

'What can I do for you?' she asked distantly, and was given a long thoughtful stare.

'Zachary asked me to talk to you.'

Maddie laughed, teeth tight. 'Oh, did he?' she asked when she could get her breath. He really was amazing! What a nerve—to get one woman to smooth his path with another!

'He told me about last night, about Con, I mean.' Jill's lips trembled; she firmed them and was silent for a moment, then went on, 'Zach didn't think you would listen to him.'

'He's right. I wouldn't.'

'Zach thinks you got the wrong impression . . .'

'I got the right one, at last. He had tried hard to give me the wrong impression until then.'

Jill looked distressed, her eyes wide and anxious, her lashes fluttering as she tried to think of some way of answering. Maddie knew she was talking in a hostile, angry way, betraying her own feelings, but she couldn't help it. Her emotion kept burning through. She watched Jill with piercing jealousy. Was Zachary in love with her? It wouldn't be surprising. She was so beautiful, and dressed like a dream. Maddie admired and could price the sea-blue jersey wool suit; she could even tell you the name of the designer. It was the style, the cut—unmistakable and very pricey. Jill knew what suited her, knew what to buy and could afford it. Maddie looked bitterly at the flawless make-up, which was smooth as enamel. She looked at the immaculate dark hair, swept up into that perfect chignon, not a strand out of place. Jill was *too* perfect, and Maddie hated her, almost as much as she hated Zachary Nash.

'No, you don't understand!' Jill protested.

'Don't I? Oh, I think I do,' drawled Maddie, pretending to smile.

Jill bit her lip at that smile, though. It wasn't very charming, more of a snarl, really.

'You see, Con has it all wrong,' Jill muttered.

'Him, too? Aren't we all sillies?'

The sarcasm drained every last vestige of colour from Jill's face, but she started to get angry, too.

'Can't you just listen?' she broke out, voice shaking. 'I must explain.'

'Don't bother! None of this has anything to do with me. I'm not involved, and you don't have to tell me anything!'

'But I do. Zach asked me to . . .'

'And you always do what he tells you?'

The gibe sent Jill's chin up. She looked angrily at Maddie. 'You've got the wrong idea about me and Zach. Yes, I'm fond of him, but not in the way you think. I've known him all my life, he's like a big brother.'

Maddie laughed; it was an ugly sound, she didn't like it much herself, and she saw Jill wince, but she couldn't stop herself acting this way. She felt cheated, she felt a fool, and resented having been tricked.

'Is that why you left Con for him? Because you missed your "big brother"?'

'I didn't leave Con for him!'

'A lot of people have told me that you left town with him. I didn't just get it from Con!'

'Zach came to collect my luggage. He drove me up to London, but he had nothing whatever to do with my reasons for leaving Con, and I certainly haven't been living with Zach since I moved to town.' Jill was flushed now, her eyes brilliant with anger.

Maddie stared at her, frowning. Jill's voice carried conviction, and why should she lie, anyway?

'Then why did you . . .' Maddie broke off, shaking

her head. 'No, sorry, I have no right to ask!'

'I was going to tell you, anyway,' Jill said in a low voice. 'Why did I leave Con? That's what you were going to ask, isn't it? I didn't want to, believe me—I love him, there has never been anybody else. But our marriage was a farce right from the start. I never saw him, he was always too busy working, that was all he cared about—the company, the job, being a success. He came home late and left early, and he wouldn't take any time off. If he had really loved me he wouldn't have left me alone so much. I was bored and fed up and very lonely, and in the end I couldn't stand it. I tried to talk to him, but he would never listen. He was too busy for that! So I decided that the only way to make him take notice of me was to leave him. I hoped the shock might make him start to think.'

Maddie stared at her, believing her. Jill's feelings were there in her eyes, in her voice, in the way her face worked.

'But it didn't work?' Maddie thought aloud.

'Oh, he did some thinking,' Jill said bitterly. 'But not along the lines I'd intended. He jumped to the conclusion that I'd left him for Zach—God knows why! I've known Zach for ever—if I had ever wanted him, I could have had him long ago.'

Maddie flinched inwardly, the words echoing in her head. So Jill could have had Zachary Nash long ago if she had wanted him? He was in love with her, but Jill had given him no encouragement? It explained a great deal that had been puzzling Maddie. It made sense of the riddle of his behaviour—if he was in love with Jill, he might have flirted with *her* to make Jill jealous.

Maddie's teeth set—who wants to be used to make another woman jealous?

'Con didn't even come after me!' Jill was saying, and Maddie looked sharply at her then.

'Did you leave a note, explaining why you were going?'

Jill shook her head.

Incredulously, Maddie asked, 'But what did you expect him to do?'

'Follow me to get me back!'

Their eyes met in silence, then Jill wailed, 'I know! It was stupid!'

'Very!'

'But I didn't expect him to simply ignore the fact that I'd gone! He didn't care if I stayed or went.'

'Of course he did!'

'Then why didn't he come after me?'

'Because he's a man!' said Maddie drily. 'Don't you know what they're like? Con's pride wouldn't let him chase after you, or let anyone see how badly he'd been hurt.'

'Do you think he was?' Jill asked wistfully, eyes eager.

'I know he was.' Con was only human. He had jumped to conclusions, and if Jill had had any brains at all she would have guessed that he was bound to jump to that particular conclusion, but Jill had been stupid, too. She had made a fundamental mistake in involving Zachary Nash in her flight from Con. Maddie gazed at her curiously, wondering if that error had been subconsciously deliberate? Could Jill really not have known how her husband felt about his half-brother, how deeply jealous he was of Zachary? Had she acted instinctively, without allowing herself to realise how she was using Zachary? Well, if she had, she had got hurt herself. Human relationships were always complicated, pondered Maddie, but especially when they were bedevilled by buried emotions. People could fool themselves so easily, as well as hoodwink others. Con and Jill had acted in a self-destructive way, but Maddie watched Jill with wry sympathy. It was so easy to be a fool; she had been one herself too often to be anything but sorry for Jill.

'What am I going to do?' Jill murmured huskily, her face working with emotion.

'It's obvious,' said Maddie. 'You must see Con, explain the truth, go back to him.'

'I can't! What if he won't listen? What if . . .'

'If you love him, fight for him,' Maddie said curtly. She knew how Con felt about his wife; he would grab Jill back, so why was Jill hesitating? I wouldn't hesitate, Maddie thought. If I loved a man, I'd do anything to get him back. Her skin burnt. If . . . she thought. What was this pain she felt whenever she thought about Zachary, if it wasn't love? Some other emotion with another name? Whatever it was, it hurt—could love hurt more? But she had only known Zachary for such a short time; this must be infatuation, short-lived but intense, a sort of sickness, a passing fever.

She vaguely let the words wash through her head, all the descriptions of love, the definitions, the latitudes and longitudes of the geography of love's territory —there were so many, but they all added up to this strange, puzzling ache deep inside her. I wish I'd never met him, she thought.

CHAPTER SIX

JILL left ten minutes later, heading for Con's flat, unless her courage gave out half-way. Maddie shut the front door on her and began automatically doing housework, her normal Saturday morning routine. It helped to have ordinary things to do; it stopped her thinking.

Zachary wouldn't be staying around here for much longer. He would leave for London and she need never see him again. She told herself how much she wanted never to see him again.

Pausing while she was vacuuming the corridor, she stared into a mirror on the wall. Her face looked disbelieving, ironic.

'I hate him!' she told it, but the expression didn't change. She couldn't even convince herself, so how was she going to convince him?

The flat was immaculate an hour later, but she still felt churned up and decided to do some shopping. How was Jill getting on with Con? Maddie wished she could be a fly on that wall.

Maybe she should have rung Con and told him to *listen*, not to be hard to convince. But Con wouldn't have wanted to hear what she had to say, he wouldn't like the fact that she knew so much about his private life, that Jill had talked to her about their marriage.

Of course, she hadn't invited Jill's confidences, had she? Any more than she had wanted Con to talk to her about his marriage! Each of them had sought her out, needing a sympathetic ear, someone neutral, who was uninvolved.

Am I uninvolved, though? she thought, pushing a trolley round the local supermarket, tossing a packet of long grain rice in here and a net bag of oranges there.

How long ago was it that Con had taken her to dinner and poured out all his troubles? She had been uninvolved then, but it seemed a very long time since—and she *was* enmeshed in the situation now. She was in it up to her neck!

She was struggling back to her flat with her arms full of groceries when someone loomed up beside her and firmly removed them all, in spite of Maddie's spluttered protests.

'They're much too heavy for you!' she was informed.

An orange rolled away and she chased after it, her face flushed from stooping—or so she told herself.

'At least it wasn't an egg!' Zachary Nash said as she furiously rejoined him, clutching the golden fruit.

'What are you doing here?' She opened the front door of her flat, but blocked his entry with her body, glaring.

He shifted the paper sacks to grasp them with one arm; the other grasped her round the waist, and Maddie beat him off, scarlet-faced and blazing.

'What the hell do you think you're doing?'

Her rage was a tactical mistake; while she was pushing his hand away he whisked past her into the flat, and the next minute was in her kitchen, dumping the groceries on the table.

Maddie hurried after him, words pouring out of her. 'How dare you walk in here without permission? Get out of my flat! Who do you think you are? I'm busy and I've got no time for idle chitchat . . .'

'Idle what?' he mocked, laughing, which didn't do her temperature much good.

'I don't want to talk to you. Just go.' She fought for icy dignity, but it didn't seem to impress him. Merely amused, he was laughing at her.

He sat down, stretching his long legs and linking his hands behind his head. She turned bitterly angry eyes on him, keeping well away.

'I mean it. Get out.' He had used her ruthlessly in his fight to get Jill, and he wasn't doing that to her twice.

His smile slowly died and his eyes narrowed, his skin darkening. 'What's the matter now? Didn't Jill talk to you?'

'Yes, she talked to me, and she told me what you asked her to tell me.' She let the biting sarcasm sound in her voice and saw it register on him, his brows flicking together, his jawline tight.

'Con has the wrong impression. Jill didn't leave him for me.'

'I know.'

He was puzzled, watching her. 'Why are you angry, then?'

She opened her lips to tell him why, then drew a shaky breath, realising that he must not know. She dared not let him guess. He was capable of taking advantage of the weakness she had for him, and he wouldn't scruple to use her, she had learnt that.

'That's my business,' she said shortly, and his frown deepened.

'I see,' he said slowly.

What did he see? she wondered, her eyes shifting and dropping. She didn't want him to have a clue about the impact he had made on her.

'Con,' he said, his voice harsh.

She was very flushed, but in surprise she glanced at him then, eyes widening.

'That's it, isn't it?' he demanded, on his feet and moving towards her. 'You're in love with Con.'

She swallowed, not knowing what to say for a second. Then, 'No, of course not!' she muttered, too late.

Zachary laughed curtly. 'I had wondered,' he said, grabbing her shoulders. 'Don't be a little fool,' he told her through his teeth, shaking her a little. 'He loves Jill, in his own short-sighted, selfish way, and if he's given you another impression, he was cheating.'

'You'd know all about that!' Maddie said bitterly, and he looked sharply at her.

'What does that mean?'

'Don't bother to ask.' She wrenched herself free and backed away, a hand up to stop him coming near her again. 'Just go away, will you?'

He didn't move, his eyes hard and glittering. 'My

God, he really got to you, didn't he?'

Thinking of him, not his half-brother, she made a wordless hiss of protest, shaking her head with violence.

'Don't pretend with me,' he said. 'What's happened between the two of you? An affair? Was he consoling himself with you while Jill was in London?'

Humiliation made her white. She turned away and gripped the sink, for support as well as to stop her hands shaking. 'Please go, can't you?' she ground out, and heard him breathing right behind her. She was as aware of his body as if he was touching her; she sensed the warmth of his flesh, the firmness of his muscles, the regular in-and-out of his breathing, the beating of his heart. How was it possible to feel all the functions of another's body when they were not even touching you?

'You'll get over it,' he said in a fiercely contemptuous voice. 'You knew he was married—what sort of fool are you? He'll take Jill back. It's over, isn't it? Has he told you it's all over? Is that why you're in such a state?'

He paused, but she didn't say a word and, after a silence, he said angrily, 'How stupid can you get, letting him drag you into this mess? Were you lovers or . . .'

'No!' she said, trembling and ashamed. He must not imagine that there had been anything between her and Con; he might tell Jill, and Maddie did not want to ruin the chance of a happy reunion between Con and Jill. 'You're imagining all this,' she whispered. 'There was no affair. Con and I have never been lovers.'

'No?' Zachary sounded incredulous. Did he prefer his own version? Was he hoping that she might yet get Con away from Jill? Maybe he liked the idea of his half-brother having an affair with another woman. If Jill ever got that idea she might leave Con again, this time for good. Did Zachary hope that she might then turn to him?

'No, there has never been anything between us,' she insisted with fierce anxiety.

'But you're in love with him,' Zachary thought aloud. 'And you've been hoping that he would start to feel the same way?'

'Don't put words into my mouth!'

'I wouldn't need to guess if you told me the truth!'

'You have no right to know anything about me!'

His voice was dry. 'You're admitting that there is something to know!'

'I'm admitting nothing! My private life is my own affair—and I want you to go. This is my weekend off. I like a little privacy at weekends. I'm in the public eye often enough during the week. I'm entitled to a little peace and quiet now and then.' She was pulling herself together, calming down. She slowly turned and could look him in the eye. His face was a shock, she had never seen it looking like that—taut and clenched with rage, all bones, his eyes deep-set and narrowed, his mouth a thin, hard line.

He tried to read her own expression, and Maddie bore the invasion with what equanimity she could muster, her chin up, her face as blank as she could make it.

He didn't say a word, just probed her face for what seemed an eternity, then turned and walked out in the same bleak silence. Maddie winced as the front door slammed, her ears echoing with the sound for ages, while she felt her whole body turning to ice. He had gone. She would probably never see him again and she wanted to cry, but she wouldn't. She fought down the pain, her eyes staring darkly at nothing.

He loved someone else, he loved Jill, she had said as much. 'I could have had Zach any time,' she had said casually, with indifference. Maddie found it hard to credit that anyone who might have Zachary could shrug him away so coolly, but Jill's very calmness had made what she said believable. She hadn't been boasting or joking; she had meant it. Zachary loved her and she was fond of him, but did not love him back.

Maddie could almost hate her, but where was the point? It wasn't Jill's fault, it was just fate, the usual ironic joke played on anyone who fell in love. It was always one-sided, or at least beset by traps and snares —look at what Jill and Con had put each other through!'

Is it worth it? she asked herself angrily as she made her lunch, a light salad of fruit and green vegetables. She wasn't hungry and only picked at it. She drank some black coffee while she read a book, trying to keep her mind off Zachary.

The phone rang half an hour later. 'Oh, hi,' she

said, recognising her sister Penny's voice. 'How is everyone?'

Penny reported on the family health and asked after Maddie's, then said, 'Maddie, are you busy tonight?' She didn't pause, quickly adding, 'I expect you've got a date?'

Guessing what was coming, Maddie said that no, she didn't have a date. 'I was planning a dull evening in front of the TV—why?'

'Are you sure? I just wondered if . . . say if this isn't convenient, Maddie, I don't want to pressure you, but we were going to the firm's dinner-dance tonight, and our usual babysitter has rung up to say she can't make it, she thinks she has got measles. And Mum can't help because she and Dad have gone to Broadstairs for the weekend to see Aunt Alice, and . . .'

'What time do you want me there?' Maddie interrupted the flow of anxious words, and Penny breathed a sigh of relief and laughed.

'Oh, you are an angel!'

'I know, you should see my wings!'

'I was really looking forward to this dance or I'd skip it,' Penny confided. 'I bought a new dress, wait till you see it, sexy isn't in it, and I'm dying to wear it and see all their faces! Dark red with sequins and a slit skirt, faintly Oriental and a very low neckline. Geoff says it's shocking.'

'Then it must be good!'

Penny giggled.

'What time, then?' Maddie asked, glancing at her watch. It was just two and a fine afternoon, if a little brisk.

'Can you get here by six?'

'Easily. In fact, I might as well do some shopping in town on my way to your place. I'll leave now and be with you in plenty of time, so stop worrying. Expect me around five-thirty.'

She was rather relieved to have an excuse for getting out of Seaborough for the weekend. She didn't want any more heart-to-hearts with Con, or his wife; from now on they could cope on their own, confide in each other. It was time they did; how could any marriage work when neither partner had much idea about the other? Con had obviously never known Jill, nor she Con. They had rushed into a marriage neither was ready for. Perhaps now they would start to understand each other?

She wouldn't think about Zachary. She made herself think about other things, anything, from the comparative easiness of driving up to London that Saturday afternoon to the prospect of a couple of hours for shopping in the narrow streets around Covent Garden, a stone's throw from her sister's little Georgian house. Penny called it Georgian but, in fact, it had been built during the building boom in London in the first years of Queen Victoria. In style it was earlier, a copy of the much-admired Regency houses in more fashionable streets.

Maddie found shopping a soothing distraction; she bought herself some delicate silk lingerie, black patent leather shoes and a very chic blue and green patterned cotton trouser-suit from a young designer with premises in the market. It was a pleasure to wander around the area, crowded with tourists and locals, in the cool spring sunshine, admiring the way the old market hall had been transformed into a shopping precinct, sitting down for a while to drink tea and watch the people flowing past. The change of scene helped to change her mood, and by the time she drove up to Penny's little terraced house she felt almost cheerful. It was good to see the family again, she missed them.

Penny had the kettle on; tea was on the table within minutes, and Penny eyed the bags of shopping Maddie had carried into the house, asking curiously, 'Anything nice? What have you been buying?' Her hair was in heated rollers, she wore a dressing-gown and old fur-trimmed slippers, her face was shiny without make-up, but she still looked lovely. Some women have all the luck! thought Maddie, letting her sister investigate the contents of the bags.

Penny loved the blue and green suit. 'I must try it on tomorrow,' she said casually, taking it for granted that she could. She and Maddie had always swapped clothes as teenagers; nothing had changed.

They were sitting in the kitchen. Geoff and the children were in the sitting-room, watching TV. Maddie had popped her head round the door and been greeted with grins all round. 'You're a life-saver,' Geoff said gratefully. 'Penny would have flipped her lid if she couldn't go tonight. Have you seen her dress? It's a disgrace.' He looked complacent, though; he liked his wife to look terrific, to make men's heads turn and people stare. He was proud of her. Geoff wasn't handsome, but he was broad and calm and very stable. Penny relied on that stability, she loved his humour and casual firmness. He was her rock; their family life was built on Geoff's strength and Penny's lively warmth.

Penny glanced at her watch. 'I've got ten minutes before I need to go up and get dressed,' she decided, and threw her sister a thoughtful look. Maddie saw it with uneasiness; she knew Penny when she looked like that. She knew the quizzing was about to start.

'So you still like Seaborough?' was the opening question of the interrogation.

'It's a nice little town.' Maddie was on her guard, wary.

'And your job's OK?'

'Fine. The show's ratings keep on rising. We're doing great things.'

'And what about you? Are you doing great things?'

Maddie shrugged, pretending offhanded amusement. 'I lead a busy life.'

'Oh? So why haven't you got a date on a Saturday night?'

Straight for the jugular! That was sisters for you! Maddie grimaced. 'I'm between men at the moment.'

'At the moment? Who was the last one? You haven't mentioned anybody since you went down there—except your boss, this Con, and . . .'

'He's married,' Maddie said hurriedly.

'I was about to say that,' said Penny. 'Didn't you say separated, though? You haven't mentioned a wife.'

'I've only just met her. They were living apart, but I think that will change soon. And before you jump to conclusions, Con is just my boss. Nothing more.'

'Is there anyone special? You've been there for six months—don't tell me you haven't met anyone.'

'I've had a few dates, but I'm not hunting for a husband. I'm too busy just now.' She hoped she sounded cool and crisp.

'I worry about you,' Penny said, staring.

'Well, don't. I'm very happy as I am.' Maddie tried to smile.

'You don't look it.'

Penny didn't mind telling the truth, even if it hurt, and she was probably accurate this time—Maddie knew she didn't feel happy. She probably didn't look it either, but she wasn't admitting anything. Zachary Nash was not a subject she cared to discuss with Penny, or with anyone, if it came to that. She meant to forget him as soon as she could, and talking about him would just encourage him to linger in her mind. He was doing that anyway, and she wanted him out: out of her life, out of her head, out of her memory.

Considering her for a moment in silence, Penny sighed and got up. 'I'd better go and get dressed. I can see I'll get nothing out of you—but don't think you've pulled the wool over my eyes, because you haven't. Something's wrong, and I'll find out what it is sooner or later. I *am* your sister!'

Maddie could find that hard to believe sometimes, and especially when she saw Penny half an hour later, a glittering vision in dark red silk which clung to her shapely body and emphasised every curve. Maddie envied her the impact of her looks; it must be nice to make men's heads turn everywhere you went.

'Be good,' Penny said to her children, and they turned wide-eyed, innocent faces up to her.

'Yes, Mummy.' Butter wouldn't melt in their mouths. Maddie eyed them ruefully and Penny laughed.

'Monsters! Now, no arguing with Aunt Maddie —you're all to be in bed by seven-thirty.'

'Yes, Mummy,' they chorused, all smiles. Maddie knew what sort of struggle lay ahead of her and sighed. She knew the three of them too well to be fooled. They had their mother's casual good looks and their father's obstinacy and will-power. The girls were the worst, actually—you could reason with Marcus, the eldest. At nine, he was a miniature adult in many ways, and had an innate sense of fairness, very English and instinctive. The only time Marcus ever got really upset was when he felt he had been treated unjustly; that burned inside him and he brooded over it. The girls, though, were twins aged six and a half: identical, delightful—and totally unscrupulous. They liked their own way and knew a thousand ways of getting it. Penny was a firm mother, but not a severe one. If the twins were a little spoilt, it wasn't Penny's fault—it was Geoff's. He adored his girls, they could do no wrong in his eyes, and Penny had no chance of teaching Angela and Kitty that the world was not their plaything because their father seemed bent on teaching them otherwise.

He was kissing them now, ruffling their curly, dark heads with an indulgent hand. 'Don't act up!'

'No, Daddy,' they said, eyes secretive and gleeful, exchanging looks Maddie intercepted with a sinking heart. What were they plotting?

'See you later, then,' Geoff said, handing her a slip of paper with a number written on it. 'You can reach us here if we're needed. We can get back in ten minutes in an emergency.'

'OK,' she said. 'Have a good time, and don't worry about us. We'll have fun.'

The children beamed, looked at each other sideways—three happy conspirators. Maddie went to the front door with her sister and Geoff and waved them off, smiling cheerfully. She sensed it was going to be a tiring evening.

She was right, and by the time the three children were in bed asleep, and the house tidy again after a couple of hours of wild excitement, Maddie was too exhausted to do more than collapse in front of the TV. She had one consolation—she had been too busy to think about Zachary.

She drove back to Seaborough on the Sunday evening in a sudden shower of spring rain, but by the time she got home the evening was mild and clear, the sea as calm as a millpond and the sky an echoing lavender blue until night rushed in to turn it deep, dark blue-black. Maddie stood at the window of her flat, watching the last wandering sandpipers probing the sand at the tide's edge.

She was both glad and sorry to be home; she found

London tiring these days, but she was tense at the prospect of seeing Zachary again. Or had he gone?

Sighing, she forced herself out of that melancholy mood and walked over to her answering machine to check if she had had any calls.

Con's voice was the third on the tape. 'Maddie, I'm going away for a few days. See you on Friday.'

He clicked off, and Maddie hurriedly rewound the tape to play the message again. Con hadn't wasted words or time, he hadn't explained anything—was he going away on business or taking a sudden holiday? Alone? Or with Jill? What had happened between them? Maddie tried to guess some answers from his voice, but it told her little except that it had a faint lilt, as if Con were happy. Or perhaps she was imagining that.

She wanted to believe Con and Jill had got together again, partly for their sake and partly because of some stupid hope of her own, but that was crazy, because it made no difference whether Jill was back with Con or not. Zachary Nash was not a man to care about, and she ought to have more sense than to spend so much time daydreaming about him. She didn't want him on the rebound, or because he couldn't have Jill.

The weather was fine and bright next day, and Maddie walked along the beach, watching the gulls swooping and soaring, wondering if perhaps it was time she moved on again, started looking for a job elsewhere. She might try going abroad. She had friends in the States, people she had worked with in London.

She felt too restless to stay here now. She bent and picked up a few flat stones and skimmed them over the waves, her face angry.

Zachary Nash had ruined her life here. Until he had arrived, she had been content and had enjoyed living in this peaceful little town, but now she felt she had to get away, start again somewhere which wouldn't remind her of him. Just seeing Con would keep reminding her of his brother; Con might not want to believe it, but he and Zachary were alike in some ways, and the similarities would keep showing through. She would never be able to forget. Yet she hadn't known him long, had she? What a difference a few days could make! Just a week ago, she had been on top of the world. Now she was angry and frustrated and restless.

She chucked the last stone with savagery, and a gull flew up with a surprised, resentful squawk, as if believing she had been throwing the stones to hit it.

'Something bugging you?'

The voice made her jump and swing round, immediately short of breath. Zachary was right behind her. She couldn't believe she hadn't heard him coming, the grate of his shoes on the pebbles and sand, but then, she had been miles away. Thinking of him. Her skin ran with hot colour. Had she conjured him up out of thin air simply by thinking about him?

'She met him first, you know,' said Zachary with something of a snap.

Maddie stared, at a loss. What was he talking about? She found it hard to care because she was absorbing the way he looked in the spring sunlight: his hair jet-black and given a bluish gleam by the sun, his body lean and tense in a cream suede bomber jacket which fitted tightly at the waist, a darker shade of cream for the trousers he wore.

'The divorce isn't final, they're still married,' he said, and then she caught on and sighed.

'Don't start that again! I'm not brooding over Con.' They were back to where they had left off before she went to London. If anything, he was even angrier, and Maddie looked briefly at him, then looked away. Was he jealous and bitter because Con had got Jill back?

'Is Jill . . .' she began and he cut in tersely.

'Yes. She went with Con.'

Maddie nodded, staring out over the sea, very aware of him standing next to her, a few feet away, his hands in the pockets of the tight-waisted jacket.

'A second honeymoon,' Zachary said bitingly, and she winced. The harshness in his voice was painful to hear.

'I see,' she murmured huskily, sorry for him and yet jealous, herself. He must really be in love with Jill to care this much. She could hear the hurt in his voice, deepening the timbre, roughening his breathing. Well, was it surprising that he should be in love with someone as lovely as Jill?

He moved abruptly, taking her by surprise. Before she had an inkling of what was in his mind, he bent and fiercely kissed her.

Her mouth quivered under the heat of his lips, the bruising demand which held no tenderness, offered no warmth, only took with ruthless force. Maddie had no chance to push him away or protest. It was over too fast.

She found herself standing alone, watching Zachary walk away across the sand, striding impatiently, his hair blowing in the wind and his footprints outlined on the wet beach. Maddie put a shaking hand to her mouth. She ought to be angry. How dared he kiss her like that? Her mouth was hot and ached. He had used her to channel his own pain and anger against Jill, and Maddie wanted to hate him for that, but she could only turn away and face the tranquil sea, tears in her eyes.

CHAPTER SEVEN

'I'M sorry!' Zachary's voice behind her made her jump again, her heart briefly stopping. 'I shouldn't have done that. I lost my temper,' he muttered. Stupidly, the admission disappointed her, which in turn made her even angrier.

'That's no excuse!'

'I wasn't making excuses, I was explaining!' He still sounded very angry and Maddie felt her nerves tighten; Zachary could be a very alarming man. Out here, on the beach, she felt that they were marooned on the rim of the world, far away from everyone else, surrounded by sea and sky, bathed in light—and yet Zachary was not dwarfed by it. He still radiated danger, power, an innate self-confidence.

She wouldn't back down in front of him, though, even if he did bother her. She faced him, chin up, eyes flashing.

'Don't you ever manhandle me again, whatever excuses you think up for doing it!'

His face was dark red, his mouth a hard line of whiteness. 'Don't take it out on me, Maddie!'

She drew an incredulous breath. He was turning it on its head again, accusing her of the very offence he was guilty of himself!

'Shouldn't I be saying that to you?'

Zachary's features tightened even more. 'You don't pull your punches, do you?'

He sounded wry now, though, and Maddie relaxed slightly, making a fist of her hand. She pretended to punch him in the stomach and he grimaced down at her.

'Be careful next time,' she said lightly. 'I might actually make contact.'

'I'm terrified.' His eyes had narrowed to gleaming slits, his lashes almost hiding them. He was half smiling and she grinned back at him.

'I should hope so too. I'm very fit.'

'I'm sure you pack quite a punch.' He encircled her wrist with one hand and lifted it to inspect her knuckles; she obligingly balled them into a fist again and he laughed.

'A dangerous lady.' He let her hand drop and looked out across the milky-blue waves. 'A lovely day.'

'Isn't it? What are you doing on the beach, anyway?'

'I saw you as I was driving along the promenade.'

'Oh, I see,' she said, watching his stark profile, frowning.

'What are *you* doing here?' he asked, and she shrugged her slim shoulders, glancing away as he looked sideways at her. She did not want him to think she couldn't take her eyes off him, even if it was true.

'I often take a morning walk along the beach on fine days.' Even on stormy days, come to that—the beach was a fascinating place in any weather. There was always something to see; after a storm or a high tide you found the most amazing things washed up on the sand: tangles of seaweed, starfish, driftwood, empty oil drums, torn clothing, old shoes, maybe a rope or a broken tool, now and then, a dead animal or a dead man. The sea brought it all ashore and left it there, like a faithful dog bringing home what it found to a master.

'You like walking?' he asked, watching her intently, as if curious about her tastes.

'Especially when I'm trying to think,' she admitted.

'About what?'

'Oh, any number of things—decisions, problems.' She had answered spontaneously without stopping to think, then became aware of his alert attention. He was probing her face again, looking for cracks in her façade so that he could find out more about her and about Con. What was he hoping to discover? That she had had an affair with Con? That Con hadn't been faithful to Jill?

'Such as?' he asked softly, and she closed up like a clam, her body tense. He wasn't finding out anything, not from her.

He watched her shrug and turn away, a slender, striking girl in close-fitting jeans and a white sweater with a cowl neck, her razor-cut black hair giving her head an elegant precision. She wasn't pretty or beautiful, but she had style, she made an impact of a different kind.

'About whether to stay on here, or move back to London?' he asked coolly, surprising her.

Her grey eyes lifted to scan his face; the sea seemed reflected in them, a diffused light that shone softly rather than with brilliance. He stood close, staring down into her eyes, but she couldn't read his thoughts in his shuttered face.

'I suppose it crossed my mind to move on,' she eventually murmured, trying to sound casual, offhand. 'In my job, we do move around quite a bit.'

'And you're a Londoner, you must miss town,' he said, encouraging her. Was he really interested in what she did, or was he still hoping to get an admission out of her, some sort of hint about her relationship with his half-brother?

She didn't miss London at all, she liked living by the sea and she liked this town, but she knew she wouldn't want to stay on here now. Her life here had been torn apart by the man standing next to her, so close and yet so far away, a stranger she knew with a puzzling kind of intimacy, a friend towards whom she felt far more than friendship, although they had only known each other such a short time.

'There are far more jobs in London in radio,' she agreed, although she thought she would probably try elsewhere, further afield.

'I have a few contacts,' he said coolly.

Maddie blinked. 'Really? In radio?'

He nodded. 'I'm sure I can get you some interviews.'

'That's very kind, but . . .'

'It's wiser to make a move at once, not hesitate or let time drag by,' he interrupted, his blue eyes hostile again.

'Don't hassle me!' she flared, resenting the tone.

'I'm not hassling you—I'm giving you good advice!'

'I'm quite capable of making a decision without advice from someone I barely know!'

His face was hard again, clenched with force, and he glared down at her as if he might hit her.

'Why are you always arguing with me?'

Maddie stared back, frowning. It was a good question—why was she?

'I can give you a list of reasons,' she said drily. 'You think you know best about everything. You're arrogant . . .'

'Arrogant?' he burst out, looking amazed.

'Over-assertive, then,' she re-worded. 'Far too damn sure of yourself—it must be the money, or did you inherit the arrogance from your father along with the money? Con said your father was a ruthless, arrogant man.'

The black brows drew together. 'Con didn't know my father.'

'He had to live with the consequences of what your father did to his mother!'

Zachary's eyes were fixed on the sea for a long moment. 'Doesn't it occur to you that my father had to live with what my mother did to him? She left him and married again—he didn't. He lived alone for the rest of his life; an embittered man brooding over the past night and day. I can understand why my half-brother feels the way he does about my father. He heard the other side of the story; he's been taught to hate my father. But you mustn't take what

Con says for the gospel truth; it's only the version of the truth which my mother and her second husband preferred.'

Maddie listened, breathing carefully so as not to disturb him, or stop him talking. She wanted to hear this, she wanted to know what his childhood had done to him, how his character had been shaped by the past. It was important to her; anything to do with Zachary was important to her. She watched his profile, tense and hard-edged, his black lashes curling back from those eyes which were bluer than the sea or sky, far more intense, with more depth and light.

'My father wasn't arrogant, but he was strong. He worked too hard, cared too much about his job, his companies. He neglected my mother, perhaps, their marriage never really worked for her. Don't think I'm saying that it was all her fault, I'm sure she had good reasons for leaving him, but he was never the inhuman monster she tried to paint him. He forced her to give me back to him, and I know that upset her. It wasn't very happy for me, either. No child likes being forced to choose between parents or side with one rather than the other. Life would have been much easier for me if my mother had never left my father in the first place, though.'

'So you do blame her?' Maddie gently murmured, and he shrugged, grimacing.

'Both of them were to blame. My father wasn't an easy man to live with, he was always away from home, flying abroad, but he expected her to put up with being left behind all the time.'

'And he expected her to put up with his other women, too, I suppose?' she said without thinking, and heard Zachary's audible intake of air.

'My God, Con didn't leave out a thing, did he?'

He was furious and Maddie wished she hadn't blurted the comment out but it was too late now.

'I'm sorry,' she said huskily. 'But it is true, isn't it? Your father did have affairs before she left him?'

'I said that she had good reasons for going. My father was no angel, but he wasn't quite as black as she painted him to Con. He didn't have a mistress or even a lover—but when he was away abroad for weeks on end he picked up girls. None of it meant anything.'

'Not to him, maybe, but apparently his wife objected,' Maddie said sharply, and Zachary shrugged.

'Oh, she found out one day and never forgave him for it. I think he did love her, though, in his way. The break-up of their marriage hit him hard. He drank in later years. He was a much harder man, too. The fight to get me back toughened him.'

Maddie softened, watching him through her lashes. He looked sombre, a big man with a hard face, yet with something indefinably vulnerable in the way his mouth was set, in the dark blue eyes and the little muscle jerking beside his lip at one side.

'You must have had a bad childhood,' she said gently, and saw him swallow, his mouth drag into a mimicry of a smile.

'It wasn't much fun, no. But my father loved me, I never doubted that.'

She remembered what Con had told her about that divorce—the vicious way it had been fought, the lies thrown at their mother. Did Zachary know about that?

'Con had a tough time, too,' she thought aloud, and heard Zachary laugh shortly.

'Con? He didn't have a problem in the world—he had two parents who stayed together and gave him a stable home. Is that what he's been feeding you? Fairy-tales about being a poor little boy caught up in a war between adults?'

His face was harsh and angry again; Maddie watched him with new understanding. She had thought Con was obsessed with the past, filled with bitterness because of his childhood—but, although Zachary seemed so much more balanced and rational about it, that was only because his angle on the situation was different. He talked calmly about his father, but he was resentful about his mother and jealous of Con. Zachary was just as obsessed with the past, after all.

'Con always felt that his mother cared more about you than about him,' she said quietly and Zachary turned disbelieving, sombre eyes on her.

'That's a lie. He can't have thought that. From the minute she married again, I never even saw her. All she cared about was her new husband, their child.' He stopped, swallowing, his face dark with anger. 'She just forgot about me.'

'No——' she began and he cut her short, his voice savage.

'Don't try to tell me how it was! I was there. You

don't know what you're talking about. You've believed everything Con told you, but then I suppose you would. You're in love with him.'

She turned to deny it, but Zachary was already gone. She watched him out of sight, his tall figure a dark pillar against the spring light, his shadow blackly floating over the sand. She had touched on a raw nerve. Zachary was a man as haunted as Con, and Maddie felt achingly sorry for both of them. They were both so wrong, so stupidly blind, and yet if you looked at it from each viewpoint you could understand why they had grown up hating each other, brooding over it all.

No doubt Zachary would be going back to London today. He had come down to Seaborough with Jill, so there was no reason now for him to stay and he must have many calls on his time in London. She knew he was a very busy man, an important man with a big company to run, but Con hadn't told her very much about his half-brother, really. Perhaps he assumed that she already knew all about Zachary? People did seem to assume that others knew things which they thought obvious. They talked in shorthand, leaving out details which might illuminate, solely because they thought them so well-known. They mystified without intending it, leaping from topic to topic without bothering to explain, quite unaware that they had left you far behind, and mostly there wasn't time to ask questions. Life moved on too fast.

Maddie slowly went back to her flat to have lunch, feeling as drained by the moments on the beach as if she had lived through an earthquake.

She wasn't sure why she felt like that—until it dawned on her that as she and Zachary talked she had finally admitted to herself that he mattered to her, that she cared about him, that the way she felt wasn't purely physical, a chemical attraction, it was more than a passing infatuation. It was love, at least of a sort.

Could you be in love with someone you barely knew? She would have laughed a week ago, shaken her head. 'No way,' she would have said. 'You can't fall in love on sight or even in a short time. Love doesn't happen that suddenly.'

But it did, if this funny, sad ache inside her was love. Was it love when you felt almost sick with excitement when someone was in the same room? When your heart seemed to flop over like a fish on dry land? When your blood sang in your ears and you felt hot and cold in turns at the sound of a voice?

She was glad to get to work that evening; having something to do kept her from thinking too much. She was half-way through the show when a caller rang to ask her to play an oldie for him. The voice made her breathing stop.

'Hello,' she said, aware of turning red. She was quite alone in the studio, nobody could see her, but she felt as obvious as a neon light on top of a building.

'Great show, Maddie,' murmured Zachary in that deep, mocking voice, and she ran a shaky hand through her hair, turning the sleek style into a bird's nest.

'Thank you. Any particular record you want?' She hoped she sounded less off balance than she felt, but she wasn't too hopeful because he distinctly laughed, softly.

'The Beatles,' he said. ' "Love Me Do".'

Maddie swallowed, and prayed that he couldn't hear her. 'OK,' she said. 'Thanks for calling. Bye.'

She cut him off before he could say anything else, and put on the disc. She had all the Beatles on tape right at her elbow, there was never a problem playing them, for people asked for them as regularly as clockwork.

So Zachary hadn't left town. Why was he still in Seaborough? Was he up to something? Perhaps he was waiting for Con and Jill to get back. Maddie worried over him for the rest of the show, and felt nervous as she stepped out of the building afterwards. The town was asleep, dark, quiet. She looked up at the starry sky and walked hurriedly to her parked car, almost as if fearing that Zachary would be lying in wait for her.

He wasn't, of course; there was no sign of him, but it seemed to Maddie that his presence brooded over the little town, a dark shadow on their skyline.

Zachary was angry and jealous and he wanted revenge—he had too many grudges against Con to be able to walk away and forget. Con had got Jill back, just as he had got Zachary's mother away from him. Wasn't that how Zachary saw it? He was staying on here until . . . until what happened? Maddie wished she knew.

She was shopping in the market square next day

when Zachary crossed the road to talk to her. She hadn't noticed him until he strode towards her, then her face drained of colour as if in some sudden shock, and she stiffened from head to foot.

'There you are!' He sounded impatient, in a hurry. 'I've been ringing you for the past hour!'

'Oh? I was out,' she stammered, still off balance, and got one of his barbed little smiles, derisive, incredulous of her intelligence.

'Obviously.'

She lowered her lashes in resentment, but couldn't help eyeing him through them. He was casually dressed in dove-grey trousers and a black leather jacket over a polo-necked red sweater—he looked vital, charged-up. His blue eyes smouldered, his jawline was taut. She shuddered inwardly, feeling that to touch him would be like touching a live wire—you would be knocked right off your feet, burned.

'I've been talking to people in London,' he said curtly. 'If you want a job, you might ring this number and fix an interview.' He pulled out a small, leather-backed notebook, and wrote some figures in it, tore out the page and handed it to her.

She looked at the number and the name below it. She knew the name at once—Peter Maddocks ran one of the new commercial stations which specialised in news and music, non-stop, day and night. She had never met him, but she had heard quite a lot about him.

'Thank you, you're very kind. It was thoughtful of you to go to so much trouble,' she said very politely, and he suddenly exploded at her, making her jump.

'Don't make conventional noises at me! Just ring Maddocks, OK?'

'Don't you bellow at me!' she snapped back, getting just as angry. Who did he think he was?

'I wasn't bellowing, just telling you.'

'Talking to me like that in the street . . .' she muttered, aware of people turning their heads to stare, grinning. She was well-known in the little town, her face often in the local newspaper, almost a celebrity, except that Seaborough didn't get overly excited about anything and would consider it ill-mannered to make a fuss in public over a disc jockey. Maddie could walk around town without being accosted, except by the occasional fan who wanted a particular record played but couldn't get through to her on the programme the night before. Now, though, townspeople were curious and amused. Did they think they were observing a lovers' squabble?

She turned on her heel and began hurrying away, but Zachary came after her and took her elbow in a commanding grip.

'Look, I'm sorry if I shouted.' His apology was a mutter, resentful, aggrieved, but Maddie slid a sideways look and was seduced into smiling at his expression. He looked like a little boy.

'You sound sorry, I must say!'

'Why are you so touchy?' he said, admitting that she annoyed him by her reactions.

'I'd say the boot was on the other foot! I was being ultra-polite and you snapped at me. You were the touchy one.'

He grimaced. 'Was I? Maybe. Sorry.' This time he sounded as if he meant it, and his sudden smile melted her heart. He had charm when he chose to use it—she couldn't resist that smile.

'It was good of you to fix this interview for me, though,' she said, relenting.

'My pleasure,' he said, pausing on the corner of the market square. From there they could both see the sea, the dancing scales of light flashing across the bay. 'Spring is definitely on the way, isn't it?' he murmured.

'Yes, looks like it,' Maddie said, gazing at the sea and sky solemnly. A week ago she would have laughed inwardly at this sparkling conversation, but her sense of humour was laid away in mothballs, it seemed. She seized on the subject with relief; it was, at least, neutral. 'I can't wait for some warmer weather.'

'Going anywhere nice for your holidays this year?' he asked, and Maddie shrugged.

'I haven't fixed anything yet. I'd like to go to China, and they're doing some very good tours there these days.'

'You like Chinese food?'

She laughed, nodding. '*Good* Chinese food,' she added after a moment's thought.

Zachary glanced down the road leading to the sea. 'What about that new restaurant down there? Have you been there? Is it any good?'

Maddie followed his glance to where a board painted with a coiled scarlet dragon swung in the wind above a newly painted restaurant façade.

'No, I haven't been in yet, but I hear the food is pretty good.'

'Had lunch?' he asked casually, and it was then that she realised where the conversation was going. She could have backed off, lied, made a polite excuse, but she felt reckless. She might regret it later, every time she saw him it seemed to make her feel worse, but she couldn't resist a chance to be with him for a while.'

'Not yet,' she said, and he made the expected response.

'Will you have lunch with me down there, then?'

'Thanks,' said Maddie, not meeting his eyes for fear of what he might read in her own. This was silly, and dangerous, but danger made her blood sing and she didn't care.

They were the first customers of the day. The restaurant had just opened, and the waiter beamed as he showed them to a table in a dark corner. Zachary had turned down a table in the window, and the waiter had looked amused, knowing. He, too, perhaps thought that they were lovers. People seemed to pick up vibrations Maddie hated to think she was giving out. *She* was so hyper-sensitive that she picked up every look, every smile, the most subtle nuances of expression or tone. She was as taut as a stretched wire; she quivered in reaction every time Zachary moved. Did he know it? The possibility made her sick. She didn't want him to guess what he was doing to her.

The food was good and they talked casually over

it, drifting from subject to subject without strain, learning more about each other. Maddie needed to know about him, she wanted to soak him up like a desert absorbing the smallest shower of rain. She was thirsty for Zachary, any detail about him fascinated her.

They kept well away from talk of family, though; any mention of Con might have wrecked the atmosphere.

Maddie discovered what sort of books he liked to read, his favourite music, food, places. He heard her views on cats, ballet, spaghetti. It was a mutual voyage of exploration; some things they had in common, in other areas they clashed, and the arguments were as enjoyable as the agreements. They grinned at each other over the table, their eyes bright. It was fun, that glance said.

'Why did you choose the Beatles?' she asked, and his eyes danced.

'You recognised my voice?'

She didn't answer, her eyes derisive, and he lazily grinned again.

'I was that generation,' he said. 'The Beatles played my music when I was in my teens.'

'I was too young to notice them until they had split up and weren't playing together any more,' said Maddie, and his eyes fixed on her.

'How old *are* you?'

She told him and he frowned. 'I'm thirty-eight. It's a big gap.'

'Not so very,' Maddie said. 'My Dad is ten years older than my Mum.'

'Is he? Do you get on with your parents?'

'We're a very happy family, very close,' she said, and saw his face darken. She had touched on the forbidden subject and Zachary was sombre.

'You're lucky,' he said, and Maddie knew she was: she had a rock beneath her feet, warmth and closeness to comfort her. Watching him, she knew then just how much his childhood had formed him. It showed in those distant, shadowed eyes, in the wry mouth. He had grown up never knowing the loving kindness of a family, the quarrels and hugs, the give and take, the compromises and discipline. He had learnt instead to take care of himself, to be self-contained and remote. No doubt it had made him grow up fast, but at what a price!

Changing the subject hurriedly, she said with a smile, 'But you mustn't keep ringing me up on the show, you know, or listeners will notice and write in to complain, and my boss will think I'm spiking the show.'

'Spiking the show?' he repeated, his face relaxing a little.

'If a show isn't doing too well, you can build up an impression that people like it by getting your friends to ring, or write, in huge numbers. It's a desperate measure and, short term, it sometimes works, but it soon becomes obvious what you're doing.' She looked at her watch. 'I'm sorry, I have to go. I've got a departmental meeting at three-thirty.'

He called for the bill and they parted outside the restaurant, Maddie hailing a taxi and Zachary standing on the pavement to watch her drive away. He hadn't suggested that they meet again. She waved, wondering if he was going back to London yet, hoping that he wasn't and yet wryly aware of the folly of becoming more involved with him than she was already.

He didn't ring her during the show, anyway. She should have been glad about that but, contrarily, she wasn't. She played mood music, melancholy blues, dreamily romantic music, thinking of Zachary and wondering if he was listening and thinking of her. He must like her or he wouldn't be spending so much time with her, or was he trying to stop thinking about Jill?

There wasn't much pleasure in seeing yourself as a cure for love for someone else.

She had been told during the afternoon meeting that her ratings had gone up over the past month. It was the sixth successive rise, and Maddie was becoming one of the radio station favourites.

'Con will be pleased,' she was told.

She asked, 'When does he get back?'

'Friday,' the others chorused, giving her funny looks, because they had already mentioned that Con was due back on Friday.'

Maddie went pink. 'Oh, yes, of course, sorry.'

'You're a bit vague,' they said, exchanging looks. And from then on they became heavily sympathetic, treating her with consideration they did not normally show her, so that she was baffled at first, wondering what was going on, until it dawned on her that they thought she was unhappy because Con's marriage was healed, and he and Jill were together again. They, like Zachary, suspected her of being in love with Con. People would jump to conclusions.

She had only just got up next morning when Zachary rang and asked her to have dinner with him.

'I'd love to,' she said, throwing caution to the winds, and spent hours shopping for something special to wear, feeling a peculiar sort of urgency, as if she was trying to make an impact on him before Jill got back and he fell under her spell again.

He drove her along the coast to a much larger town; they ate at a very expensive, very fashionable restaurant specialising in French cuisine. They talked and looked at each other with such fixed attention that Maddie hardly noticed her surroundings, though; she had no idea who else was in the room or even precisely what she was eating.

He had such long eyelashes, thick and black, brushing his cheek just above the angle of the cheekbones. Now and then he looked down and she stared, then saw the glint of his eyes through the lashes, the curl of his mouth, amused by her stare, so that she flushed and he looked up and smiled at her.

He knew, she thought, her heart beating, breathing thickly—he knew she was falling for him. Was that a smile of amusement? Or did he feel the same way?

Hope flared inside her, but she couldn't forget Jill. She wouldn't let herself be such a fool.

He dropped her at the radio station in good time, but she found it hard to concentrate on her show. The music was right in mood, but Maddie hated talking, making jokes, thinking . . . she just wanted to drift with the music and dream.

He rang her while she was still in bed next day. 'Oh, hello,' she said, stretching sensually under the fine cotton sheets.

'What are you doing this morning?' he asked, and Maddie laughed softly.

'At the moment, I'm still in bed.'

'Are you, then?' he murmured, after a silent pause, his voice husky. 'Did I wake you up? I'm sorry.'

'I was awake,' she explained. 'I felt too lazy and comfortable to get up, though.'

'Why bother?' he agreed. 'Stay where you are and I'll be round in ten minutes.'

She laughed as if he was joking, but wondered— was he? Her breathing quickened at the very idea and her face became flushed.

'Why did you ring?' she asked hurriedly, flustered.

His voice had an amused note. 'To ask you to lunch.'

'Oh,' she said, smiling.

'And dinner,' he added.

'Today?' Her heart was crazily jumping about.

'Yes.'

'Both lunch and dinner?'

'Yes,' said Zachary, his tone low and intimate. 'Why not breakfast, too, as you haven't got up yet?'

'I'm not eating breakfast today, and I've got a lot to do this morning, but lunch would be nice.'

'And dinner?'

'We'll discuss it over lunch,' she said, feeling light-headed and very happy.

She was waiting for him, dressed in a new cream wool dress, and aware of high excitement, when the phone rang and his voice made her collapse inwardly.

'I'm sorry, Maddie, I've had an urgent summons to London and I'll have to break our date, I'm afraid.' He sounded brusque, impatient, as if part of him was already en route for London and absorbed in work.

She tried not to let her feelings sound in her own voice. 'Oh, what a pity. Well, never mind, some other time,' she said with controlled and automatic politeness.

'I'll be back,' he said—but would he? 'See you,' he added and she echoed the words.

'See you.'

The phone clicked off, and Maddie slowly hung up. She would not cry, even though she felt like it. Depression settled on her like low cloud, making the whole world misty.

At least she still had her job, and she was grateful for that. She kept busy; her flat shone with polish, everything in its place, neat and tidy. She read, went to the cinema, drove out into the surrounding countryside, swam at the local indoor pool, visited the riding stables and took a horse out for a couple of hours. There was plenty to do in Seaborough; sport and leisure was well provided for because the little town was a seaside resort and visitors liked ways to amuse and occupy themselves.

She didn't hear from Zachary, though. By Friday morning she had given up hoping. Zachary was back in his own world and he wouldn't be returning to Seaborough. She faced that fact and tried to convince herself that it was not going to blight her life if she never saw him again. He was just a might-have-been that had become a memory.

Con walked into her office that Friday evening, while she was getting the show together. Maddie didn't hear the door open and jumped sky-high when his voice spoke right next to her.

'Busy?'

She spun in her chair, heart thudding. 'Oh, Con, it's you. You made me jump!'

'Sorry,' he said, grinning.

'You're back,' she said and he nodded.

'You noticed!'

She laughed. 'Sorry, I'm just surprised to see you.' For a stupid, blindingly painful second, she had mistaken his voice for Zachary's. They were alike, not very much, but enough for her to think in that first startled flash that the voice was the one she wanted to hear. Hope could betray you into stupidity, she admitted ruefully.

'I said I'd be back today.'

'Yes, so you did,' she said. 'Have a good time?' Her eyes asked other questions—was everything OK between him and Jill? Was he happy? Was the marriage whole again?

Con looked down into her eyes, smiling, answering silently. Yes. Oh, yes, he was happy! He looked entirely different, a man she had never met before. Con had been deeply unhappy when they had first met and, indeed, throughout the whole six months she had been working here. She hadn't known him before his marriage had broken up and so she hadn't realised until now how much difference unhappiness had made to him. His face was so often bleak and grim, his temper harsh and impatient. Now he was relaxed and carefree, the lines of his face smoothed out.

'How's Jill?' she asked tentatively, smiling.

'She's fine—we're moving back into our house this week. It will keep her busy for months, she says—she plans to do a lot of redecoration.'

'I'm so glad,' Maddie said warmly. Even if she hadn't been rather over-sensitive at the moment, she would have been struck by the change in him, but she was the more alert to it because she was entering the same dark waters. Zachary had gone away and he hadn't rung or written. If he had cared at all for her, wouldn't he have got in touch? She probably wouldn't see him again, and one day she might be able to accept that calmly, but at the moment she was bitterly depressed. It was like looking through a dark window at a cold world, on which the sun would never shine again.

'Thanks, Maddie,' Con said, sitting on the edge of her desk, folding his arms. 'So, how's the show coming along?'

'Tonight's show is about settled,' she said,

handing him the running order she had worked out. He read it, then nodded.

'Sounds great. Any good letters?'

She nodded, gesturing to the little pile she had sorted out from the rest, and Con sifted through them, skimming a line here, laughing or frowning. One reason for his success was his interest in every aspect of his business, his understanding of the problems and his grasp of essentials. Maddie liked working for him.

'Well, I must get on,' he said at last. 'I've left Jill asleep. She was exhausted by the travelling, but I was wide awake so I thought I'd try to catch up on my paperwork.' Con got up and Maddie stared at him incredulously, laughing. 'What's funny?' he asked.

'Work? At this hour?'

'Perfect,' he said gravely. 'Nobody around, peace and quiet for once—no interruptions. Couldn't be better, in fact.'

'I think you miss your work when you're away from this place!' she half accused, still amused.

'Just between you and me, I do,' he admitted ruefully. 'I'll be working late, so play one of my favourites, will you?' He told her the piece he wanted, and Maddie promised to play it and did so during the show that night, wondering if Con was listening or if he had become so absorbed in work that he had forgotten all about her.

She was just leaving after the show when Con appeared again and grinned at her. 'Wonderful show tonight! I heard it all—it made a nice background noise while I worked.'

'Thanks, that's just what I like to hear—a nice background noise is what I've always wanted to be.'

Con had a bottle under his arm and two glasses held by their stems between the fingers of one hand. 'Champagne,' he said, as Maddie eyed them. 'A celebration—from what Jill tells me, I owe you a bottle of champagne and a vote of thanks.'

'You don't owe me a thing,' she protested, rather pink.

'Jill says I do. She tells me you set her right and sent her back to me.' Con was smiling as he put the glasses down on the desk in the studio office, and then began carefully easing the cork out of the champagne. 'We talked for hours and I saw what a stupid, blind idiot I'd been—too much imagination, that's my problem. I'd built my half-brother up into a threat and it was all in my own mind. Jill was never in love with him at all. As she says, if she had wanted him, why would she have picked me? Just because he has been around all her life doesn't mean there has ever been anything between them. Jill has never been attracted to him, that's the truth.'

'I realised she still loved you the first time I met her,' Maddie said gently. 'It was as clear as daylight.'

The cork popped, the champagne fizzed, and Con hurriedly poured it into a glass and then filled the other.

'Very expert,' Maddie teased him, laughing. He lifted one of the glasses and held it out to her, lowered his head and kissed her lightly on the mouth. 'Thanks, Maddie. More than I can say.'

She ruffled his hair offhandedly. 'Just be happy, Con.' She couldn't get over the change in him; the glow in his serious hazel eyes. Con was a different person, one she yet had to learn to know.

'I am,' he said deeply, then picked up his own glass and raised it in a toast. 'That's our toast—to happiness.'

Maddie lifted the glass to her lips, smiling, then out of the corner of her eye caught a movement by the door. She began to turn and saw Zachary's lean figure in a dark suit, his face hard and unsmiling, his narrowed eyes hostile, viciously blue.

Her heart seemed to stop, her breathing a rasp in her lungs, then she turned fully and he was gone. The door swung softly, but she heard no footsteps and she had a moment of panic, of confusion. Had she imagined it? Had he really been there?'

'What's the matter?' asked Con, frowning at her, obviously having seen nothing.

'Nothing,' she said slowly. My mind is going, she thought. I'm starting to see him when he isn't there. He's haunting me, and I wish he would stop.

It was half an hour before she and Con said goodnight in the car park. She drove home slowly, her mind inert and heavy, filled with a grey misery over Zachary which she couldn't dispel. There was a faint mist over the sea. Somewhere a foghorn moaned and the waves murmured and whispered over the sand with melancholy persistence. Maddie locked her car and stood staring at the empty, cold beach, shivering although there was no wind and the air was quite warm.

A footstep behind her made her jump and turn, shaken. Not again, she thought with drowning panic, expecting to see some man lunging at her.

There *was* a man, big and dark and threatening, but it wasn't a stranger. Maddie almost wished it was.

'Zachary!' she whispered, shaking at the angry contempt in that face. She hadn't imagined she saw him in the office tonight; he had been there and he was staring at her as if he hated her.

'I almost turned and went back to London,' he said through his teeth. 'Maybe that's what I should do, but for Jill's sake I'm not walking out on this squalid little game. You may think you're going to be able to hang on to Con, even though Jill is back with him, but you can forget that. You aren't staying down here and carrying on with your affair. You're leaving Seaborough and staying away from Con, and I'm going to make sure you do!'

CHAPTER EIGHT

MADDIE was outraged, her face a scalding red as she stared at him incredulously. 'You're crazy, do you know that? Not a word of that is true, and even if it was it wouldn't be your business.'

'You're not making Jill unhappy all over again,' said Zachary with biting hostility.

Jealousy ground inside her and she had trouble controlling her voice and face. 'Jill isn't your concern. It's time you saw that.'

'I don't understand you,' Zachary snarled, and she saw a light come on in the downstairs flat just behind them.

'Don't shout at me,' she muttered, seeing the curtain twitch and a face show briefly. 'Do you know what time it is? You'll wake the whole street!'

'As long as I make you listen, I don't give a damn,' he said just as loudly, and Maddie saw another light come on in another flat.

'For heaven's sake,' she whispered, 'why didn't you bring a megaphone? Some of them haven't heard you yet.'

'You're coming up to London to have that interview with Maddocks,' he said, ignoring what she had said.

'Oh, shove off!' Maddie snapped, but he caught her as she turned to walk off, shaking her with hands that hurt. She fought, glaring, her black hair dishevelled, flung across her face in wild strands. She saw him through them and was torn between fury and a stupid, helpless attraction.

'I hate you,' she muttered, trying to kick him.

'Not as much as I hate you,' he said, and her body flinched in pain, although surely she hadn't been dumb enough not to know that he didn't even really like her?

She kicked him hard, and Zachary said something violent and shook her, so she kicked him again and found herself grabbed towards him. She stumbled on one leg like a stork, mid-kick, and toppled forwards. Her head hit his chest. Under her ear she heard the thud-thud of his heart. She had wondered if he had one, but it belonged to Jill, so why should she care anyway? It sounded very loud and rough through the well cut waistcoat of that expensive suit; it sounded, in fact, as if he had been in a race and lost.

'You're squashing my nose,' she said nastily, wriggling, but his arms were tightly wrapped around her and she was a prisoner.

'God knows why I drove like crazy to get here from Heathrow in time for the end of your show,' he said with his chin resting on her hair. 'I've been in transit for around ten hours now, and I feel half dead, so don't push me, Maddie.'

'Where have you been?' she asked, distracted by curiosity.

'Los Angeles. An urgent business matter. I put it through at top speed so that I could get back as soon as possible. I tried to ring you a couple of times, but the line was busy.'

His arms were so tight that she couldn't breathe, and she ached to give in and lean, cling, put her arms round him, but she wouldn't because it was Jill he cared about and he was only using her, so she pushed and struggled, her breath sobbing in her throat.

'Damn you, stand still!' he said, controlling her with hands that hurt. It was a dangerous little war that they were fighting, and Maddie wasn't even sure she knew which side was which. Touching him even in anger made her skin burn and her body shake, and their movements were like gestures in some primitive ritual: wild and drenched with longing, intensely sensual.

They both heard the wail of the siren as the police car came round the corner. Headlights blinded them, and they fell apart, staring as the car drew up and two policemen jumped out and ran towards them. One was tall and fat, the other short and thin. They both had the same alert, suspicious expression.

'What's all this, then?' one said. 'Are you all right, miss?'

She nodded, puzzled for a second, until it dawned on her and she almost laughed out loud, realising what they thought.

'We had a report that there was a disturbance,' the tall, fat one said, rubbing his chin thoughtfully as he watched her. 'A lot of noise, fighting in the street —people got woken up. It is the middle of the night, you know, and we've had some very serious incidents lately.'

The short, thin one said hopefully, 'Was this man threatening you, miss?'

She slid a sideways look at Zachary, almost tempted to say yes, but finally shook her head. 'We were arguing, that's all. I'm sorry if we disturbed people.'

They did not seem convinced. Sharp-eyed, watchful, they asked, 'Are you sure, miss?'

'Of course I'm sure. Why should I lie about it if I was being attacked?'

'Oh, people do the funniest things when they're scared,' said the fat policeman. 'If you're being threatened . . .'

'I'm not!'

'If you were, though, you wouldn't need to worry about reporting it. You'd get protection, don't worry.'

'I'm not being threatened or attacked. We were quarrelling. I know him,' Maddie said, but realised that it was almost funny that, if she chose to be vindictive, she would get Zachary into quite a tight spot, and from the wry set of his mouth he knew it. She hoped he was nervous.

The policemen scowled from her to Zachary, glancing at each other with irritable faces. 'You can get yourself into trouble, you know,' said the fat one, 'causing a public disturbance in the middle of the night! Wasting police time. Waking up all your neighbours. Why don't you both go home?'

'Sorry, officer,' Zachary said, and took Maddie's arm to lead her away, but at that moment the fat policeman said sharply, 'Hang on!'

They both looked round and he stared at Maddie. 'Don't I know you?' He clicked his finger and thumb, exclaiming, 'I know! You're the girl who was attacked the other day!'

Maddie turned pale at the memory. 'Yes,' she admitted, and both policemen studied her openly, their faces professionally interested.

'After what happened, I'm surprised to see you out so late at night, miss,' said the fat policeman. 'I'd have thought you'd be too nervous.' Their eyes held suspicion again.

'I work at night, I have to go out,' she said.

'Oh? Doing what?'

'She's Maddie,' Zachary said tersely, and they both looked at him. 'On the radio, you must have heard her show!' he told them.

The fat one said, 'Yes, I remember now,' but he was studying Zachary closely. 'I've seen you before, too, haven't I? You aren't the guy who . . .'

'No!' Maddie said shrilly, her whole body shuddering, although why the question should disturb her she couldn't have identified.

'I drove Miss Ferrall to the police station for the identity parade,' Zachary said, his face and voice icy. 'That may be where you saw me. Do you want to see identification, officer?'

Something in that face, that authoritative tone, changed the whole atmosphere. 'No, no, that's all right, sir,' they said, backing off. 'But no more noise, please. Go home and have the argument there.'

They drove off and Maddie breathed again, shaken by the incident somehow, perhaps because it had reminded her of that other night, the terror and sickness she had endured. Zachary had been kind, then, and she had been grateful to him for the strength and support he offered her. It seemed a very long time ago now. In a short time so much had happened to her.

'I began to think we'd never get rid of them!' said Zachary, and she threw him a resentful look.

'You can go, too.'

She walked away into the flats and he kept pace with her. 'I still haven't finished talking to you.'

'That's what you think.' Maddie inserted her key into the front door. 'Goodnight.'

He blocked the door with his foot so that she couldn't shut it. 'Do you want the police back again?'

She eyed him, seething. He was capable of making another scene so that her neighbours should call the police back. 'We haven't got anything to say to each other,' she said, but as his mouth opened she stepped back crossly. 'Oh, come in, then—I'm very tired, you know. It's the early hours of the morning.'

Zachary consulted his watch. 'Ten to three,' he agreed, closing the door behind him. 'We mustn't wake your neighbours up again, must we?'

'You're lucky I didn't bring charges after you attacked me just now!' Maddie muttered resentfully, walking into the kitchen.

'*I* attacked *you*?' he repeated, following her. 'I'm the one who's black and blue. You're a violent woman.'

'If I am, you make me violent!'

'Do I now?' he asked, his voice dropping to an intimate murmur, his eyes narrowed. She felt her insides melt and resented that, too. Why was she so weak about this man? She had never been weak towards any other. To cover her reaction she sat down by the table and looked at him coldly.

'What was it you wanted to say that is so urgent?'

He picked up the kettle and filled it at the sink before he answered. 'I want to make arrangements about this interview with Maddocks. I'll fix it and I'll drive you up to London.'

'You'll do nothing of the kind!' she snapped. 'What are you doing with that kettle?'

'Making tea—I need a cup, I don't know about you.'

'I want to get to bed!'

'Why not? I'll make the tea and bring it along,' he drawled, and she bared her teeth at him.

'I didn't find that funny the first time, and I'm getting sick of it now. Will you please go?'

'Are you hoping to wreck Con's marriage again?' he asked abruptly, his face harsh, watching her as if he had hoped to surprise an admission.

She said angrily, 'No, no, *no!* I told you, I'm not interested in Con. I'm glad he and his wife are together again. This whole thing is in your imagination, not mine.'

'Then prove it—come to London and see Maddocks.' He spoke coolly, but he watched her like an enemy, a weapon trained on her heart.

Maddie was too tired. She couldn't go on fighting. 'Oh, OK,' she said flatly, drained. 'Anything to get rid of you. I must get some sleep.'

She felt him considering her and closed her eyes, sighing wearily. A second later Zachary was beside her, stooping. Her eyes flew open in shock. He picked her up like a child, one arm under her legs, the other at her back, and she was too startled to protest or resist.

Her head lay on his shoulder, and she lay limply against him as he carried her to her bedroom.

He laid her down on the bed and sat beside her. 'Are you too tired to undress?'

'No,' she said, stiffening, ready to beat his hands away, but he simply grinned at her.

'Pity—sure?'

'Go away, Zachary,' she said, and he bent and kissed her lightly. She had an intolerable desire to kiss him back, to put her arms around his neck and pull him down with her on to the bed, to touch him with exploring hands and discover the muscled flesh his expensive suit covered, but still managed to suggest. He dressed like a city animal, but her senses told her he was the jungle variety and dangerous.

'I'll ring you at eleven—can you be up by then, do you think? And then if Maddocks can see you I'll pick you up half an hour later,' he said absently, then kissed her again, not so lightly, with probing insistence, and her whole body burned.

'Stop it,' she whispered, her hands on his shoulders, pushing him away, even though she really wanted to slide her hands inside his smooth shirt and stroke his skin.

'Stop tempting me, then,' he whispered into her throat, kissing his way downwards.

'I'm not doing anything of the kind!' She knew she should be feeling more insulted, but she was simply too tired, and she was enjoying the soft slide of his lips on her skin.

'Lying there, looking at me with half-shut eyes,' accused Zachary, lifting his head to watch her.

'I am not.' She tried to open her eyes wide, but she was so sleepy . . . Zachary leaned over and softly tickled her lashes with the tip of his tongue. Her eyes closed entirely. 'Don't,' she said on a groan, and then his mouth came down hard. Her lips parted on another groan and the warmth of his tongue caressed the tender inner skin of her mouth.

'I need this,' he said thickly, and she heard the piercing excitement in his voice and recognised it for the mirror of her own desire. But, she reminded herself, Zachary was in love with Jill, and only using her to comfort himself because he could not have the woman he wanted. Maddie was wrenched between the fierce needs she felt herself, and her sense of personal integrity. She could not let him make love to her when she knew it wasn't her he wanted, even though she wanted him so badly. It would torment her afterwards; she would hate both herself and him.

She broke free and angrily fought him off. 'Leave me alone! Don't try to touch me!' Her voice held incipient hysteria, a rising shrillness which he recognised. His hands dropped and he sat up, frowning, brushing down his hair and straightening his tie.

'It's OK, Maddie, don't panic,' he said gently. 'Stupid of me not to realise you might, so soon after that damned attack.'

She sat with her back to him on the other side of the bed, breathing rapidly, roughly, and didn't answer.

'I won't rush you. We have all the time in the world,' Zachary said. 'Goodnight.' His fingers lightly trailed down the curve of her spine and she shivered helplessly, then he was gone and she heard him walk towards the front door, heard it open and shut quietly. Maddie rolled over on to her face and cried into her pillow, her body aching with yearning and frustration.

She slept like that, without even waking up to undress, and woke up stiff and cold in broad daylight to find that it was half-past ten. She stared incredulously at the clock and sat up, her head banging. She felt as if she had a hangover, and she looked at herself with distaste. She had slept in her clothes and they were creased and crumpled. She felt creased and crumpled, too.

She stripped and had a shower, the lukewarm jets tingling on her hot skin and waking her up. The phone rang as she was towelling herself, and she knew who it was and didn't hurry to answer it.

'Did I wake you up?' asked Zachary without identifying himself.

'No, I was just having a shower.'

'Sleep well?'

'I slept,' she said unrevealingly, not intending him to know that she had dreamt all night, as far as she could remember, and of him. They had been Technicolor dreams, hot and unreal, while at the same time intensely real, so that she was appalled by the power of her own imagination.

'Are you still in a temper?' he asked drily.

'Did you get in touch with Maddocks?' she countered, without bothering to answer that.

'Yes,' he agreed, his voice wry. 'He'll see you this afternoon at three-thirty, which gives us plenty of time to drive to town and have lunch first.'

'I can drive myself to town, thanks,' Maddie said curtly. She really preferred not to see him after what she had been dreaming about him. It might show in her face!

'I'll pick you up in half an hour,' Zachary merely told her.

'Now, look . . .' she burst out furiously, but she was already talking to the empty air. He had hung up. Maddie slammed her own phone down. 'Obstinate, maddening, interfering,' she muttered to herself as she went to get dressed. 'Who does he think he is, pushing me around all the time?'

Viewing herself in the mirror, she comtemplated her reflection with acidity. If only she was as fabulous-looking as Jill! She would love to make Zachary Nash rock on his heels!

She hated everything about the way she looked—her nose was too short, her eyes that boring, ordinary grey, her face certainly wouldn't launch a thousand ships. It probably couldn't even launch one! Her figure was neat, but didn't make men swoon in the street. What had she got? She groaned, wishing she was tall and sexy with long, long legs and full, ripe breasts, then she feverishly ransacked her wardrobe for something spectacular to wear—but what?

She picked out a flame-red silk shirt and a black velvet skirt with a tight waist. At least she looked vivid in it, faintly gypsyish with her razor-cut black hair and a flame-red lipstick on her mouth. She gave herself more height with very high black patent shoes, but still wasn't happy with her reflection. There was nothing more she could do about it, though, so she crossly sprayed herself with perfume and then went to make some coffee. She wasn't hungry, but the strong black coffee helped her to think. She sat with it, brooding, curled up on the sitting-room couch with a mug clasped in her hands, frowning at nothing.

Zachary might not have her interests at heart when he insisted that she should leave Seaborough, but it would be her best decision, anyway, and it would be a career step up to start working for Peter Maddocks. She was really quite excited about meeting him. He was a big name and had a lot of influence.

Zachary must have influence, too, she thought, her eyes sharpening. How had he talked Maddocks into seeing her?

She was curious about Zachary's business connections—Seaborough gossip hadn't been very informed about that, but then, what they had told her about Con and Jill and the break-up of their marriage hadn't been exactly accurate, had it? Anything you were told by a third party or outsiders had to be taken with a pinch of salt. Seaborough talked about Con a lot, but really didn't know a thing.

I ought to warn Con that I'm thinking of changing my job, of course, she thought. When I get back from London I'll talk to him—or maybe I shouldn't say a word for a while? I'll tell him if I get a job. After all, Maddocks may not like me—or I may not like him! I may not be interested in whatever work he has in mind for me. Anything can happen, and there's no sense in talking to Con until I have more idea about the future. I would just upset or annoy him for no good reason, and once he knew I was thinking of going he would never feel the same again. Our working relationship would be torpedoed. A boss never likes to know that an employee is job-hunting elsewhere.

It was really maddening that her life had changed so drastically overnight. One day she had been as happy as a sandboy in Seaborough, and planning to stay for years, and the next she was desperate to get away, too restless to contemplate spending any more time in Seaborough.

Con would be baffled. A startled look came into her grey eyes and she frowned at a new thought.

I hope Con doesn't suspect I'm leaving because of him! He might, of course. It could look that way—he wouldn't guess it was because of Zachary. Why should he? He would only see that she had been perfectly contented here until he and his wife got together again.

It was bound to look like that to him. What else could explain her abrupt change of heart?

Maddie's face was hot as she contemplated his probable expression when she told him. She knew she would stammer under his startled eyes. Con would look embarrassed and uneasy. She would go red and tongue-tied. He would look sorry for her, but eager to get away because he wouldn't know what to say or do —and when he told Jill that Maddie was leaving, Jill would get suspicious, too.

Very soon, half Seaborough would believe she had been in love with Con and had gone away to nurse a broken heart!

Maddie ran her hands into her hair, groaning. How stupid! She couldn't let them all believe that. It was too embarrassing.

What she needed was an excuse, she realised, some reason for going which was plausible enough to convince Con and Jill and everyone else. But what?

Then it came to her in a flash, and she sighed in relief, her grey eyes clearing. It was obvious once she thought of it—simple and obvious, totally convincing.

Family reasons. Penny needed her living nearby—Con knew how close a family she came from and he would accept that. All she had to do was work out why Penny should suddenly need her close at hand—because she was ill? Having another baby?

She would work that out, anyway; it wouldn't be hard to think up some very plausible reason.

The doorbell went and she jumped, her heart beating so hard that it hurt.

Zachary, she thought, her mouth dry and her skin burning. On the way to the door, she looked at her face in the mirror, wondering if it showed, this violent reaction to him. Could he read it in her face?

She didn't know whether to be glad or disappointed that she looked almost normal—if you didn't notice the feverish glitter of her eyes or the flush in her face, or the faint trembling of her mouth.

Zachary did, of course, as she might have known he would. Those shrewd, narrowed blue eyes skimmed her face the instant she opened the door.

'Feeling nervous?'

Her eyes were startled. She swallowed, not knowing what to say, and he smiled down at her, his mouth warm.

'No need to be, Maddie. You'll like Maddocks, he's a nice man and he won't be tough on you.'

She sighed with relief as she realised how he had misinterpreted the cause of her tension. 'Glad to hear that!' she muttered as they walked out into the sudden shower of spring rain.

They ran to the car and Zachary unlocked it. She hurriedly climbed into the passenger seat, and a moment later they were on their way.

'How did you meet Maddocks?' she asked as they drove out of Seaborough and headed for London.

'My firm made most of the electronic equipment the radio station uses.'

'Of course!' she thought aloud, wondering if he had made the equipment in the studios at Seaborough. How did Con like that?

'But I first met Maddocks when he interviewed me years ago—he was doing a series of programmes about industry, and I was one of his targets—or guests, if you prefer.' He grinned. 'At the time, I felt quite definitely that I was a target. Maddocks didn't pull his punches, he's a good interviewer.'

'You're making me nervous, again,' Maddie said, and he shot her a quick, concerned look.

Maddie's heart contracted. Why did he have to be so nice? She wished she could hate him. It would make life so much easier.

'That's different, he's not going to be gunning for you,' Zachary said.

She wasn't so sure about that later that day when she faced Peter Maddocks across a wide desk covered with scripts and letters and piles of documents. He looked formidable enough to her: a tall, thin man in a grey-striped suit and dark tie, he had hawklike features; sharp-nosed, quick-eyed, alert, ready to swoop down if you were unwise enough to break cover.

'Tell me about yourself,' he had said at the beginning, and she had burbled helplessly, not sure what he wanted to know but giving him an outline of her career to date. It sounded unimpressive; she hadn't done very much at all, had she? Peter Maddocks' yellow-brown eyes commented in silence.

He asked questions which were terse and to the point. Maddie answered uneasily at first, and then got angry and began to snap.'

'Why do you want to change your job now?' she was asked, and before she could answer, 'You say your ratings have gone up consistently, so when you've only been there six months it seems puzzling that you should want to move on so soon.'

'Personal reasons!' she said curtly.

'Ah,' he murmured, thin mouth cynical. 'Mr Nash, I assume.'

Maddie flushed to her hairline, her eyes opening wide. It was only then that it dawned on her how it must look, and what Peter Maddocks thought. Zachary had talked him into seeing her, perhaps against his will. If he jumped to obvious conclusions about her relationship with Zachary, who could blame him?

'No,' she said angrily. 'I have family reasons for wanting to move to London, to be near my sister, in fact.'

Maddocks looked politely unconvinced. 'I understand,' he said blandly.

'Look, I don't want any special favours because of Zachary!' she burst out.

'Your private life really isn't relevant. I'm sorry I mentioned it,' Maddocks said, soothing her.

Humiliated, Maddie bit her lip. 'I just want to be judged on my own ability!'

'You will be,' he assured her. 'Zachary is someone I respect, though—he has a nose for talent.'

What sort of talent did he mean, though? she fumed, looking away and wondering what else to say. If this man thought she wanted to come to London to be with Zachary, what would Con think when she told him? Would everyone leap to the same conclusion?

Maddocks leaned over and switched on a tape machine; her own voice filled the room to her surprise. She looked sharply at the man on the other side of the desk, who smiled.

'Zachary thoughtfully provided a tape.'

She hadn't thought of bringing a recording of her show. She should have done; it was a stupid lapse of professionalism.

'I've listened to it several times,' Maddocks said in that dry voice. 'I like your technique—natural and easy, but controlled, good choice of music, quite a nice little show.'

'Thank you,' she said, watching him and wondering what he really thought, not to mention whether she really wanted to work for this man. Zachary had said he wasn't tough; Zachary had not told the strict truth! Maddocks knew his business, though. She might not have impressed him, but he had impressed her. If he did offer her a job, she would be a fool not to take it.

'I'll let you know,' he said when she left half an hour later, and she still had no idea what he thought of her or whether he would offer her anything.

Zachary had suggested waiting for her and driving her back to Seaborough, but she had decided to go to her sister's and stay there that weekend. She had told Zachary she would get the train back on Sunday night. He had asked her for Penny's address, and she had refused to give it to him. She was very glad about that now. If Maddocks imagined she was having an affair with Zachary, it might not be entirely a piece of deduction.

Zachary might have told him so. And what if Zachary planned to turn his little piece of fiction into fact?

Maddie's teeth met as she drove across London in a taxi to her sister's house, staring out broodingly at the spring sunshine. Zachary Nash could think again —he wasn't buying her with this job with Maddocks!

CHAPTER NINE

MADDIE had to talk to someone, and it had to be someone who wouldn't rush off to tell the rest of the world her secret. She had plenty of friends, several from schooldays, but this was one secret she couldn't trust to anyone but her sister. Penny wouldn't gossip. Of course, she would feel free to comment with her usual frank brutality. They had, after all, known each other all their lives, and Penny had always felt free to say what she thought about Maddie's behaviour. She had criticised her friends, her clothes, her posture, her taste, her schoolwork, her men. Penny regarded her sister as one of her possessions—of little consequence, of course, since she certainly did not expect to get frankness back from Maddie and would be insulted if she did, but still *her* sister and in a way under her protection.

Maddie hesitated that weekend, but she had to make a decision, and to do that she had to confide in someone, see the problem from all sides, from outside herself.

Penny was only too happy to listen. Maddie chose Sunday morning, while they were cooking family lunch together and Penny's husband was in the garden with the three children, building a bonfire behind the vegetables.

'Is he good-looking? He sounds very rich,' said Penny, fascinated, washing small new potatoes in her sink. Geoff had just come in with a trug full of freshly dug vegetables from their garden, before going off to have his bonfire.

'I told you, he's in electronics, and I suppose he is good-looking.'

'You suppose?' Penny chuckled teasingly, and Maddie went pink.

'That's beside the point, though.'

'I'd say it's very much to the point. Chop the mint for me, would you? It's the first of the season.'

'Mmm, smells gorgeous,' Maddie said, sitting down at the table to start chopping the green sprigs on the chopping board. 'All I wanted was advice from you about changing my job—do you think I should, when I've been at Seaborough such a short time?'

'If you get a better offer, why not?' Penny was always practical, and Maddie grimaced, admitting she was right. 'I knew something was going on down there!' Penny said triumphantly, drying her hands and looking around the kitchen, her brow wrinkled.

'Nothing is *going on*, as you put it! What are you looking for?'

'Where did Geoff put the broccoli?'

'It was in the trug.'

'I know that—but where's the trug?'

'It was here a minute ago.' They both looked around, then Penny gave an impatient yelp.

'There it is, by your leg, under the table—honestly, Maddie, why did you put it down there, out of sight?'

'Sorry!' Maddie said ruefully—in the wrong again!

Penny had a genius for making her feel guilty. She pulled the flat wicker basket out from under the table, and Penny seized it.

'I can always tell when you've got something on your mind,' she said, sitting down at the other side of the table. 'Or I should say *someone!*'

Maddie was pink, she wished she hadn't started this conversation. She should have kept her mouth shut. 'Anyway,' she said defensively, 'even if Maddocks doesn't offer me a job, I definitely think I'll come back to London. I'll never enjoy living in Seaborough after all this.'

'You mean you want to be in London where you can see Zachary,' Penny bluntly said, and Maddie took a long, harsh breath, turning crimson.

She couldn't get out a word, but she made miserable, protesting noises, shaking her head.

Penny laughed. 'Oh, don't look at me like that! You know it's true.'

'No,' Maddie said, thinking, is it? Is that the truth? Did she feel this urgent haste to get back to London because she wanted to be near Zachary?

'Of course it is!' Penny shrugged. 'If being in Seaborough would remind you of him, why move to London where he *lives?* You'll both be in the same city then. And if, according to you, Con Osborne hates the sight of his half-brother, Zachary isn't likely to be visiting Seaborough very often in the future, is he? Be logical, Maddie.'

'Look, the idea didn't even enter my head!'

'You didn't want to face it, you mean! But that's the reason, all the same—the mating instinct.'

'Nothing of the kind!'

'You're after him,' Penny said wickedly, and Maddie growled in her throat.

'I am not!' Maddie had to change the direction of this conversation. Hurriedly, she said, 'I haven't felt safe in Seaborough since I was attacked, actually.'

Penny's face altered at once, concern in her eyes. 'I'm sure you haven't. I can understand that, I'd be having nightmares.' She patted her sister's shoulder. 'And we want you back in town, although heaven knows, none of us feels exactly safe here, either. But this is where your family are and where you belong, close to us . . .'

'And available for babysitting more often!' Maddie said drily, and her sister laughed, unabashed.

'Well, there is that! You come back, Maddie.' She got to her feet. 'How about coffee? We've done all the chores, and we won't be serving up for another hour.'

Lunch was a cheerful, noisy meal—after the roast lamb came plum tart, made with bottled plums from the tree in the garden, and after that coffee for the adults, while the children stowed the washing up into the dishwasher in the kitchen. Geoff talked lazily about his garden, and Penny listened intent with uneasiness to the sounds in the kitchen, ready to leap to her feet at the first crash. 'I know they're going to break something!'

'Then why let them do it? I'll go and finish loading the machine, shall I?' offered Maddie, getting up.

'No, they have to learn,' Penny said. 'Sit down, Maddie.'

Maddie couldn't sit still. She prowled around the

room, looking at framed photographs and ornaments. The décor had been chosen to fit the architecture; the furniture was traditional, charmingly suitable. She admired the wallpaper, fingered the striped brocade curtains.

'Why are you so restless?' asked Penny.

Maddie looked out of the window, sighing. 'Oh, Sundays are so dull,' she said, looking at the narrow London street of nineteenth-century houses. Nothing was happening out there; everyone was indoors or in their gardens.

'Waiting for someone?' Penny enquired, watching her with wry amusement, and Maddie went red again. It was infuriating to be so transparent. Why was her sister so shrewd and quick to notice things?

She looked out of the window again, but this time a car was driving down the quiet street and her heart clutched inside her.

She must have made a sound because Penny got up. 'Is it him?'

'Him? Who?' Maddie stupidly gabbled, and Geoff looked up from his lazy contemplation of the Sunday papers.

'What's all this? Is there something I should know?'

'When there is, I'll tell you,' Penny assured him and he laughed.

'Women!'

Back in her own flat that night, Maddie couldn't sleep. She didn't know why she should have been expecting to see Zachary all weekend, especially since he had not even known where she was, but with total lack of logic, she had, every waking minute.

Being in love was tedious, she thought, turning over again and thumping her pillow.

Who had invented it? Not women—it had to be men, the game was weighed in their favour, they got the best of it.

When she went into work next day, Con rang down to the studio to ask her to come and see him. His voice was brusque; he sounded irritable, and Maddie wondered what was wrong now.

She soon found out. 'What's all this about you applying for a job behind my back?' he threw at her before she had sat down on the other side of his desk.

Maddie stiffened, flushing. 'How . . .'

'Peter Maddocks rang me—did you forget to ask him not to?'

The biting sarcasm made her wince. 'I'm sorry, Con. I was going to tell you . . .'

'When? When you got the job?'

She bit her lower lip; it was only too true and she couldn't deny it.

'I thought you liked it with us,' Con said, sounding baffled and upset. 'You're doing so well, and you've only been here six months—why do you want a change? I suppose my half-brother talked you into it? Typical of him, poaching my staff! He always wants what other people have got.'

'Poaching your staff? But . . .'

'You must be blind if you can't see what he's up to!' Con ground out, dark red with rage. He was wearing an elegant blue-striped suit, but he had flung off his jacket, unbuttoned his waistcoat, rolled up his shirtsleeves, taken off his tie and opened the collar of his striped blue and white shirt. He looked like a man getting ready for a struggle.

Bewildered and uneasy, she stammered, 'Con, I don't know what you're talking about, but I'm afraid I must . . .' She was about to start on her prepared explanation that she had to move back to London to be near her family, but Con didn't let her finish.

'He's furious because Jill has come back to me, so he's trying to hit back at me through you!' he almost shouted.

'Through me?' Her grey eyes darkened in shock. What was he saying?

'Stop repeating everything I say! It's quite simple, do I have to spell it out? He can't have Jill, so he's decided to steal my top people away. These big London set-ups often go out into the provinces to head-hunt, where else do you think they find their new talent?'

Maddie couldn't believe what he was telling her. She swallowed hard. 'Are you telling me that Zachary is behind the London company that controls . . .'

'Of course!' said Con, staring hard. 'You mean you didn't know?'

'All he told me was that he had supplied equipment to them!'

Con laughed harshly. 'I'm sure he did; he certainly wouldn't offer that contract to anyone else, would he? He owns a hefty slice of the company shares—through one of his companies!'

Maddie stared at nothing. 'He lied to me!'

'He's a liar, what did you expect?' Con's eyes were

hard, though. 'Why did you want to go, Maddie?' he asked, frowning.

She shrugged. 'I don't know, I've been feeling odd the last couple of weeks.' She couldn't meet his eyes; she felt her dismay over Zachary must show in her face.

'I suppose it was the attack on you,' Con slowly thought aloud, and she seized on the idea.

'Yes, I don't feel the same about this place any more. I want to go home.'

'London's a hundred times more dangerous!' he protested.

'But it's my home town.'

'And you're bolting back to it? Well, I suppose that's understandable, but will you do me a favour, Maddie? Think it over first. We don't want to lose you. You're becoming very popular.'

'Am I?' she asked, distracted by the professional compliment and smiling.

'If it's a question of more money——' Con murmured with reluctance, his eyes cagey.

She laughed. 'Don't look so wary—it isn't! More a question of wanting to feel safe again.'

'In London?'

His irony made her smile, but it was a mere pretence of amusement. She was too shaken by what she had just discovered. Zachary had deliberately told her that lie—why? Why hadn't he wanted her to know he controlled the radio station in London?

She knew why, though—the fact changed the whole picture, didn't it? He hadn't simply got her an interview with an old friend. He had told Maddocks to see her. He had probably told him to give her a job. The set-up was totally phoney, and so was Zachary Nash.

Maddocks rang her at home next day, just as she expected, and offered her a job—it was a very attractive offer, too: good pay, a late-evening show of the same type as the Seaborough show, but ending at midnight rather than starting at it. If Maddie hadn't known that Zachary was behind the offer she would have leapt at the job, but as it was she politely turned it down.

Maddocks was taken aback. 'No? Don't you want to think about it before you give me an answer? I'll be writing to you with the formal offer. Wait until you get my letter before . . .'

She was firm. 'I've changed my mind, I'm not leaving my current job.' It might be foolish to miss this chance of getting a start with a London station, but she couldn't help suspecting Zachary's motives in tempting her away from Con and Seaborough. She didn't trust him, and she'd like to know exactly where she stood before she made such an important change. There would be other chances later. She would rather stay in Seaborough for the moment, and she told Con so as soon as she saw him. She was going to learn to forget Zachary Nash if it killed her, and her sister was quite right—she wouldn't do that in *London*, where he lived!

Con's explanation had been very convincing, and Maddie believed it implicitly, even though it hurt.

Zachary was jealous of him and wanted to hurt Con any way he could, and snatching popular people from

Seaborough Radio was a shrewd business move as well as a blow at Con. He could get his own back and profit by it, too. Very clever, she thought bitterly, mouth awry.

It should be flattering to know that he saw her as important to Con's operation, someone Con would regret losing—but she was too sick to care. It had been bad enough when she thought Zachary was persuading her to leave Seaborough because he wanted to protect Jill's happiness, but to discover that instead he had been using her as a weapon against his half-brother was humiliating. It made her feel ill.

When would this childhood vendetta of theirs end? It was destructive to both of them, why couldn't they see that? They weren't unhappy children any more, they were adults—it was time they started behaving like them and put childhood things away.

It was destructive to those around them, too, of course. Jill had suffered from this feud. So had she. Her ego had really taken a beating when she realised that Zachary saw her as a tool, a mere pawn in this private little wargame.

After Maddocks rang, she sat back to wait for Zachary to explode back into her life. Maddocks was bound to get in touch with him at once, to tell him she had turned the job down, and Zachary would want to know why. She had every intention of telling him—and she couldn't wait to do it!

He didn't ring that afternoon or evening. Maddie spent the time in a state of agitated suspense, constantly working on epithets to hurl at him, insults to sling, home truths to tell.

By the time she fell asleep in the early hours, after her show, she was feverish with expectation. She kept waking up in the night, her head full of whirling words, having dreamt that confrontation.

The next day dragged: she looked at the clock every two minutes, she jumped when the phone rang, she stood at the window in her flat, looking into the street and watching for his car.

He didn't come and he didn't ring her at the radio station, either. She couldn't believe it. Hadn't Maddocks yet informed him? Was he indifferent anyway? Wasn't it at all important, whether she took the job or not?

She felt like a timed bomb which hadn't gone off; she was loaded with explosive and frustrated as hell.

'Why are you talking to yourself?' Con asked her in the lift, and she started, staring at him blankly, having hardly noticed him join her on the ground floor.

'What?'

He repeated his question, looking amused.

'Talking to myself? Was I?'

'Well, muttering under your breath—rehearsing, are you?'

She pulled a tight smile from somewhere. 'Yes,' she said, and it wasn't a lie because she *was* rehearsing, she was going through what she would say to Zachary—if he came. If he ever came.

By the end of the week, she was drained; exhausted by the strain of being wound up for so long without ever getting the chance to snap. She slept late on Saturday, but it wasn't a restful sleep. She was too miserable and had had bad dreams, none of which she could remember when she did wake up.

What woke her was the telephone ringing, and she shot out of bed and stumbled, running to answer the phone, barefoot, flushed, trembling.

If it was Zachary at the other end she probably wouldn't be able to get out what she had been rehearsing to say to him all week. Her nerves had completely gone; she was witless, stammering.

Her hand snatched at the phone, and she gabbled the number, but as the phone reached her ear she heard the dialling tone and knew that whoever had been ringing had hung up.

Maddie put the phone back and stood there, almost in tears. What the hell is wrong with me? she asked herself, furious now. So, whoever it was has given up waiting! If it's important they'll ring again—and it probably wasn't him, anyway.

She went into the kitchen in her short cotton nightie and put coffee on, let up the blind and winced at the spring sunshine flooding into the tiny room.

Another day. She turned her back on it. She preferred night; she was an owl, a night person. Night was safe, secretive, silent. She sat and waited for her coffee—she wasn't hungry, she couldn't eat. She hadn't eaten much for days. Her appetite had gone. Another crime to be added to Zachary's sheet. It was his fault. Everything was his fault.

Why am I letting him do this to me? she thought resentfully. Why let *him* ruin my appetite or my life? She would *make* herself eat. She hunted out muesli, poured it into a bowl and looked into the fridge for milk, but there was none left. She had used it up on cocoa the night before, hoping it would help her sleep.

The milkman would have left today's pint by now, so Maddie trudged to the front door to get it. She bent to pick up the carton, and that was when she heard footsteps: quick, striding footsteps. From under her lashes, she glanced that way and her heart stopped.

She should have leapt back into the flat and slammed the door on him, but the shock of seeing him there made her too slow-thinking.

She straightened, clasping the carton, flushed and breathless and with a racing heart now.

Love was lethal, she thought: an illness whose symptoms were even worse than what caused them. Her heart was so erratic, she wondered it worked at all. She ought to see a specialist, but which doctor could advise someone whose physical reactions were so wild and unpredictable? She'd end up with a psychiatrist—no sound medical opinion could doubt her insanity! Poor creature, they would think. Mad, quite mad.

'I want to talk to you,' Zachary said as he reached her, and Maddie eyed him in what she hoped was an icy manner.

'I have something to say to you, too. You lied to me! Why didn't you tell me that your company owned that radio station? But that's obvious, isn't it? Do you know what you are? You're a . . .'

She stopped short, not because he frightened her, although there was menace in his face, but because one of her neighbours had opened a door and was staring at them, fascinated by the sight of Maddie in her nightie, having a noisy row with a man on the doorstep.

Maddie was embarrassed and pulled a grimace of a smile into her face. 'Oh, Mrs Perkins! Good morning.'

'Nice day, isn't it?' the neighbour answered, obviously without any intention of going back indoors while something interesting was happening out here.

Zachary pushed past Maddie, and she reluctantly had to let him into the flat, pausing to smile politely at her neighbour before she shut the door.

She found him in the kitchen, pouring himself coffee. Glaring, Maddie slammed the carton of milk down on the table.

'I don't want you in my flat. Get out!'

He leaned on the sink, coffee in one hand, while with the other hand he unbuttoned his cream leather bomber jacket. He didn't say anything, but his eyes made her flinch. He was an alarming man and he was even angrier than she was.

'I've had enough of you!' she snapped.

'You haven't had me at all yet,' he said, and watched her face burn while he took his time looking her over from head to foot, his blue eyes hard and narrowed and insolent.

She had never been so conscious of her own body in her life—or so intensely aware of a man's. Zachary's eyes explored and travelled over the nakedness of her legs and arms, her bare shoulders, the half-concealed breasts whose pale, smooth skin showed through lace and ribbons, the hard, raised nipples to which the thin cotton clung.

'You should get dressed before you open that front

door,' he told her absently, without lifting his eyes. 'Or at least put on a dressing-gown.'

'That's what I'm going to do now,' she said, backing to run away.

'Not yet,' he said, catching hold of her with one peremptory hand.

Maddie yanked to get free, torn between sensual awareness of him and fury.

'Why didn't you tell me that you had shares in that company?' she muttered, and he shrugged.

'I didn't want to confuse the issue.'

She curled her lip at him. 'The truth might have confused me? Well, there's a novel excuse for lying!'

'I had a suspicion that if I told you, you might not go for that interview.'

'You mean I'd have guessed you were up to something!'

'I wasn't up to anything that I'm ashamed of—but that's exactly the reaction I thought I might get if I told you the whole truth. It's nonsense, of course . . .'

'Oh, of course!' she echoed derisively, and he scowled at her, his face taking on that fugitive likeness to Con suddenly which always surprised her when she noticed it.

'The only fact that mattered,' he snapped, 'was whether you were good enough to interest Maddocks!'

'You ordered him to see me, and no doubt to give me a job!'

'I did nothing of the kind! I've got my money invested in that place—how long do you think the company would survive if it employed people without talent? I have my shareholders to consider. They expect to make a profit, and if the audiences dwindled so would the advertising. If I hadn't thought you could do the job, I wouldn't have suggested you to Maddocks—but I assure you I didn't lean on him. I gave him a tape of your show, that's all.'

She stared, wondering if she could believe him, beginning to think he was telling the truth.

'Now,' he said on a deep breath, holding her eyes, 'why did you turn the job down? To stay here? Near Con?'

She didn't answer for a second, and his long fingers tightened around her wrist, making her gasp.

'You're hurting!'

'Then tell me the truth. Did you decide you couldn't bear to leave Con?'

'*You're* obsessed with your half-brother, I'm not!' Maddie said angrily. 'Look, get this into your head—I am not in love with Con. I have never been in love with Con. I have never even remotely felt I *might* be in love with Con. There's nothing between us, never has been, never will be.'

He watched her intently, still frowning, a dark, angry man with violently blue eyes, and Maddie wished she could say the same about him as she just had about Con. She didn't want to be so fiercely attracted; it was hard to think when he was there, and that made her feel stupid.

When he didn't say anything, she said impatiently, 'You know, you and Con have the same problem. You apparently can't forget what happened when you were children. Isn't it time you stopped feeling sorry for yourselves and grew up?'

'This has nothing to do with that,' he said then, still scowling. 'If you aren't in love with Con, why have you turned down this job?'

'Because I won't be used as a weapon against anyone,' she snapped. 'In fact, I won't be used. Full stop.'

'Used? What are you talking about?' He looked furious but baffled, and Maddie wished she knew whether or not he was acting.

'You know very well! Why are you so keen for me to leave Seaborough? You want to protect Jill, get me away from Con, you said . . .'

'That's part of it,' he admitted, eyes half closed, considering her through the slits in a wary way which made her very suspicious.

'Are *you* in love with *Jill?*' she attacked, hoping to surprise a betraying look out of him.

In a sense she did—he looked amazed! 'In love with Jill?' They stared at each other in silence for a moment, then he asked slowly, 'Now, what gave you that idea? I've known her since she was a toddler; we lived next door to each other for years, I thought I'd told you that. Jill could almost be my sister, and that's all there is to it.'

The relief was so intense that it felt like pain, and Maddie could have cried out with it. She couldn't stand, her legs were so shaky. Hurriedly turning to the nearest chair, she sat down while Zachary watched her. She didn't like the way he did it, or the little smile on his face.

'Don't loom,' she muttered. 'I haven't had breakfast yet. I haven't even had coffee, come to that.

I'm suffering from low blood sugar or something.'

'Or something,' he said softly, still observing her face with interested blue eyes, and Maddie knew she grew even more flushed, but he did then pour her some coffee. Their hands touched as she took the mug and her body vibrated. If she wasn't so angry with herself she could have noted her odd physical sensations with scientific curiosity, but she couldn't summon up the right mood.

'Did you really think I was in love with Jill?' he asked, sounding almost amused and certainly shrewd. Zachary was doing some thinking, and she wished he wouldn't. She hunted her mind for something to distract him, without being able to come up with anything. She wasn't thinking too clearly.

'You . . . you said something about wanting to get me away from Con, though,' she said. 'For Jill's sake.'

'I said that was partly true—I'm fond of Jill, and I want her to be happy, but that wasn't my main reason for wanting to get you to London.'

'Then what was?' she asked, holding her coffee in both hands to disguise the way her fingers trembled.

'You mean you still don't know?' he mocked, taking the coffee from her and putting it firmly back on to the table.

'You were using me to annoy Con?' She resisted his attempt to pull her to her feet.

'I wasn't using you!' he impatiently denied. 'That's crazy—who put that into your head, or can I guess? Con? Look, I don't hate Con the way he seems to hate me. I barely know him, but whenever we do meet he's so hostile, he makes me angry, too. I'm no plaster

saint, I react like any other human being—if I find
myself being attacked, I hit back, but, aside from that
natural reaction, Con doesn't really figure much in my
life at all. I don't spend all my time brooding over him
or over the past. I agree with what you said about
forgetting what happened so long ago. I have. It seems
to be Con who can't.'

Her grey eyes hunted over his face; it was hard and
impatient, but she read honesty in those features.

'Can we forget him now, and concentrate on more
important things?' asked Zachary, his hands sliding
down her arms, the warmth of his palms caressing her
cool, bare skin.

Her heart beating too fast, Maddie got up. 'I'd
better go and get dressed,' she muttered, her eyes
down.

'Not yet,' he said, his hands closing on her waist
before she could get away. 'We seem to have spent too
much time at cross purposes, Maddie. I want you in
London, where I can see you all the time.'

'Oh!' she said, taken aback and incredulous—did
he mean it? Taking a long, deep breath she asked,
'Why?'

Zachary laughed, his blue eyes tender, teasing. 'I'll
show you why.' His head began to come down towards her, and she could hardly breathe at all now.
She drowningly watched his mouth, her eyes darkening with desire, but it was all happening too fast.

'Wait!' she said, scared rigid by the urgency inside
herself. 'Don't, not yet, I must think . . .'

'Think later,' he said in that warm, husky voice,
which had first attracted her the night he'd rung her

during the show and told her that he was a stranger. It had been so true; again and again since then she had been forced to realise that Zachary *was* a stranger. Even now she wondered how much she knew about him, how well she would ever know this man, who had come so close, and bewildered and tormented her so much. She loved the sound of his voice, she wanted him to go on talking to her while she got control of herself again, but there was something else she wanted even more. She wanted him to kiss her with a fever that made her freeze one minute and burn the next. It was like being delirious.

'Don't rush me,' she pleaded, and he laughed again, because that was just what he meant to do—rush her.

'Maddie,' he whispered, almost against her mouth. 'Oh, Maddie,'

She closed her eyes at the note in his voice, the hunger and excitement. Her arms went round his neck, and their mouths met eagerly, the passion making her head whirl. She had thought she loved him, but now she saw she had been deluded—she hadn't even begun to know what it was to love until now.

'I've been crazy about you, ever since I first saw a photo of you in the local paper,' he said, holding her so tightly she could barely breathe. 'It was fuzzy and hard to tell what you looked like, but for some reason I switched on that radio to listen in to your show, and I loved the sound of your voice. You were funny and quick with it, and I knew I had to meet you. I think I knew right from the start that you were going to matter to me.'

She ran her fingers into his thick, warm hair and looked up with half closed, drowsy eyes, her mouth aching with the long kisses. 'I wish you'd told me you were Con's half-brother, right at the start, though—we wouldn't have misunderstood each other.'

'Maddie, it didn't occur to me for a while that you didn't know. I'd told you my name; I hadn't tried to deceive you. How was I to know you hadn't any idea who I was? You knew I was down here with Jill.'

'I've been stupid,' she said, making a face.

He kissed the tip of her nose. 'I won't argue with that.'

She laughed. 'Con was so sure you were in love with Jill.'

Zachary's mouth twisted. 'I have more sympathy with him now that I know how it feels to be afraid every other man in sight is after the woman you want yourself.'

Her colour deepened, her eyes glowed. 'Jill *is* beautiful.' There was a faint, lingering uncertainty in the way she watched him, and he smiled down at her, the violent blue eyes filled with a feeling that she could not mistake, and which sent her blood singing through her veins.

'Of course she is, but I'm too used to her to notice now, any more than I notice the wallpaper in my office.'

Maddie couldn't help smiling at the thought of Jill as mere wallpaper, and he watched her with amused comprehension.

'I see you like that idea! Isn't that typical of a woman?'

'I like Jill, but not when she might . . .' Maddie broke off, very pink.'

'Might?' he queried delicately, eyes teasing. 'Want the same man?'

'Don't put words into my mouth!'

'My plans for your mouth don't involve talking,' he said, and kissed her for several minutes without giving her a chance to say a word.

'Oh, Maddie,' he whispered later, 'you've given me a hard time the last week.'

'*I* gave *you* a bad time? How do you think I felt? You didn't get in touch. I didn't know if you even cared whether I took that job or not.'

'I cared,' he said grimly. 'But I'd had to go abroad again. I can't just drop everything at a moment's notice. I've had to make time to see you, and it hasn't been easy.'

'You could have rung!'

'Oh, no, not this time—I had to be there, able to see your face, touch you.' He slid his hands down her back, his cheek against her hair. 'I needed this, a little real contact. I won't pretend you're the first woman I've ever wanted, but you are the first I've ever thought I loved, Maddie.'

She stiffened in his arms, going white, then red. '*Loved?* You're going too fast! We're almost strangers—can you love a stranger?'

'I don't know, Maddie,' he said wryly. 'In fact, I don't know much about love at all. I only know how I feel about you. No face has ever haunted me the way yours does—I'm always thinking about you. Nothing else seems to interest me much any more. I saw the face of a total stranger in a newspaper, a pretty fuzzy picture at that, and that started it all. I had this strong feeling that I wanted to hear the voice that went with it, so I turned on the radio and heard your voice, and suddenly I couldn't think of anything but meeting you. From the first, the way I felt was that immediate, that violent, so I suppose the answer is yes, Maddie. You can love a stranger.'

She had listened gravely, her eyes still unsure. 'It's crazy,' she said, and Zachary laughed, his eyes tender.

'Is it?'

She leaned on him to kiss him. 'Quite crazy—and I am, too, because I feel the same. The minute I heard your voice, when you rang up during my show—I think I knew. There and then was when it happened—a stranger's voice and I was as tense as if I was on trial for my life. I didn't know who you were, or anything about you, but you really got to me before I even saw you.'

'At least we're crazy together,' he said, his mouth in her hair, whispering the words. 'And you must come to London, Maddie. I don't want to be away from you ever again. I want you with me all the time.'

She trembled at the depth of feeling in his voice, her eyes closing, but common sense made her protest. 'But, Zachary, what on earth can I say to Con? I promised him I wouldn't leave—he'll be furious.'

'It may finally get it through that thick head of his that he's always had the wrong idea about me and Jill,' Zachary merely said. 'But whatever Con thinks, does it matter? Forget Con, can't you? I can. I have more important things on my mind.'

His fingers slid down her throat, found her chin and tilted her head back. His face was poised above hers, the dark face of a stranger, and yet bewilderingly familiar from the very first. Maddie looked at him with love and desire, her grey eyes misty. He didn't need to tell her what was on his mind; she knew, because the same obsession gripped her, too. She stood on tiptoe to meet his mouth, and he was right—nothing else mattered.

Enjoy one beautiful romance after another this holiday.

A holiday provides the perfect opportunity to immerse yourself in a heady new affair and with the Mills and Boon Holiday Romance Pack you'll be spoilt for choice.

In this special selection you'll find four brand new novels from popular writers Emma Darcy, Sandra Field, Jessica Steele and Violet Winspear.

The collection is unique as well as being excellent value for money and will slip easily into your suitcase.

We think you'll find the combination irresistibly attractive.

Just like so many of our leading male characters.

Published July 1988.   **Mills & Boon**   Price £4.80.

Available from Boots, Martins, John Menzies, W H Smith, Woolworths and other paperback stockists.

BRIGHT SMILES, DARK SECRETS.

BEYOND THE RAINBOW

She lived in a glittering world of high fashion, where power, jealousy and even murder fed white-hot fires of passion

MARGARET CHITTENDEN

Model Kristi Johanssen moves in a glittering world, a far cry from her small town upbringing.

She carries with her the horrific secret of physical abuse in childhood. Engaged to Philip, a top plastic surgeon, Kristi finds her secret a barrier between them.

Gareth, Philip's reclusive ex-film star brother, has the magnetism to overcome her fears.

But doesn't he possess a secret darker than her own?

Available July. Price £3.50

W RLDWIDE

Available from Boots, Martins, John Menzies, W.H. Smith, Woolworths and other paperback stockists.

YOU'RE INVITED TO ACCEPT **FOUR ROMANCES** AND A TOTE BAG **FREE!**

Acceptance card

| NO STAMP NEEDED | Post to: Reader Service, FREEPOST, P.O. Box 236, Croydon, Surrey. CR9 9EL |

Please note readers in Southern Africa write to:
Independent Book Services P.T.Y., Postbag X3010, Randburg 2125, S. Africa

YES! Please send me 4 free Mills & Boon Romances and my free tote bag – and reserve a Reader Service Subscription for me. If I decide to subscribe I shall receive 6 new Romances every month as soon as they come off the presses for £7.50 together with a FREE monthly newsletter including information on top authors and special offers, exclusively for Reader Service subscribers. There are no postage and packing charges, and I understand I may cancel or suspend my subscription at any time. If I decide not to subscribe I shall write to you within 10 days. Even if I decide not to subscribe the 4 free novels and the tote bag are mine to keep forever. I am over 18 years of age   EP20R

NAME _____
(CAPITALS PLEASE)

ADDRESS _____

_____

_____ POSTCODE _____

Mills & Boon Ltd. reserve the right to exercise discretion in granting membership. You may be mailed with other offers as a result of this application. Offer expires 31st December 1988 and is limited to one per household.
Offer applies in UK and Eire only. Overseas send for details.

They were survivors, both of them... But could they overcome the scars of war?

THE FLYING MAN

Ann Hulme

They were survivors, both of them. But they had survived scarred...

In post World War One Paris there is a new era, full of hope and determination to build a brilliant future.

Alix Morell is one of the new young women, whose strong will and new-found independence helps her face the challenges ahead.

Jake Sherwood is a Canadian pilot who had fought his way to the top - but whose dreams are shattered in one last cruel moment of war.

Can Alix release Jake from his self-made prison?

Their compelling love story is poignantly portrayed in Ann Hulme's latest bestselling novel.

Published June 1988　　　　　　　　　　**Price £2.95**

W●RLDWIDE

Available from Boots, Martins, John Menzies, W H Smith, Woolworths and other paperback stockists

SPOT THE COUPLE
AND WIN A
£1,000
REAL PEARL NECKLACE
PLUS 10 PAIRS OF REAL PEARL EAR STUDS WORTH OVER £100 EACH

A

B

No piece of jewellery is more romantic than the soft glow and lustre of a real pearl necklace, pearls that grow mysteriously from a grain of sand to a jewel that has a romantic history that can be traced back to Cleopatra and beyond.

To enter just study Photograph A showing a young couple. Then look carefully at Photograph B showing the same section of the river. Decide where you think the couple are standing and mark their position with a cross in pen.

Complete the entry form below and mail your entry PLUS TWO OTHER "SPOT THE COUPLE" Competition Pages from June, July or August Mills and Boon paperbacks, to Spot the Couple, Mills and Boon Limited, Eton House, 18/24 Paradise Road, Richmond, Surrey, TW9 1SR, England. All entries must be received by December 31st 1988.

RULES
1. This competition is open to all Mills & Boon readers with the exception of those living in countries where such promotion is illegal and employees of Mills & Boon Limited, their agents, anyone else directly connected with the competition and their families.
2. This competition applies only to books purchased outside the U.K. and Eire.
3. All entries must be received by December 31st 1988.
4. The first prize will be awarded to the competitor who most nearly identifies the position of the couple as determined by a panel of judges. Runner-up prizes will be awarded to the next ten most accurate entries.
5. Competitors may enter as often as they wish as long as each entry is accompanied by two additional proofs of purchase. Only one prize per household is permitted.
6. Winners will be notified during February 1989 and a list of winners may be obtained by sending a stamped addressed envelope marked "Winners" to the competition address.
7. Responsibility cannot be accepted for entries lost, damaged or delayed in transit. Illegible or altered entries will be disqualified.

ENTRY FORM

Name _____

Address _____

_____

I bought this book in TOWN _____ COUNTRY _____

This offer applies only to books purchased outside the UK & Eire.
You may be mailed with other offers as a result of this application.